In Exile

Billy O'Callaghan

MERCIER PRESS
Cork
www.mercierpress.ie

Trade enquiries to CMD Distribution,
55A Spruce Avenue, Stillorgan Industrial Park,
Blackrock, County Dublin.

ISBN: 978 1 85635 598 8

10 9 8 7 6 5 4 3 2 1

A CIP record for this title is available from the British Library

the arts council an chomhairle ealaíon Mercier Press receives financial assistance from the Arts Council/An Chomhairle Ealaíon

Printed and bound in the EU.

This book is dedicated to Liam and Regina, my parents, whose support and encouragement means the whole world to me. To my brother, Martin, and my sister, Irene, and to the memory of my good and much-missed friend, Andy.

'Reality leaves a lot to the imagination.'

– John Lennon

On The Road

And when all the fuss died down
Lazarus began to feel
His old aches and pains return,
And he yearned for sleep
For he was mightily tired.

Later in the day,
And feeling a little better, he sat
With Christ and asked him
Whether he ever felt weary
And hopeless
On the road.

'Only as a man,' replied Christ
With a smile, stretching
As he rose
To stir his sleeping scribes.

– Andrew Godsell (1971–2003)

CONTENTS

THE BODY ON THE BOAT

Nobody noticed the body until the boat had docked for the evening at the pier in Gull's Bay. A light squall had muddied the sky and even here, already moored, the twenty-four feet of vessel heaved relentlessly to port with the beat of the swell.

Finnegan had come up from below and he stood on the arrow point of the bow feeling for the intentions of the weather. Down below deck, giving the engine a routine service ahead of tomorrow's venture out into the Sound, there had been little evidence of any storm threat except the movement, like a cradle on a bough. Not much noise even; the world beyond the moaning flank walls muted but for the clap of the *Bella Vista*'s rim colliding again and again with the pier's stanchion poles. But up here at the boat's helm, exposed to the full roar of the ocean, it was like a different day.

The brackish water churned with ill intent, the broken, heaving surface pocked with scuds of white, pulled asunder by a directionless rising gale. Already darkness was coming down, the deceptive early night of a storm, but for now the eerie twilight held, foretelling the menace of things to come. A storm that would rage all night, a bad one that would drive the boat against the pier, tear at the rope bindings and planking of deck and hull. Escape from total destruction lay in the lap of the gods, and Finnegan didn't much rate their chances. All they could do was give in to it, to throw themselves at the mercy of ocean and sky, and take whatever punishment that came.

There was much work to be done in this last hour of half-light, the boat to be secured and the day's catch to be gutted and put on ice, but still he lingered a while at the helm, glad of the sense of isolation. Alone with the heave and sigh of the ocean, breathing the air hard with sodium. He loved the emptiness of the moment, the torment of the wind crashing against the water and that odd siren cry that seemed to seep upward from the very depths, and then, better, the sudden shift in the wind's direction that would bring a stillness, just a heartbeat of it, a thing filled to bleeding with anticipation, like all the world was taking pause in readiness for the next onslaught.

His reverie was shattered by the shouting of Lavery, one of the crew. Finnegan turned, at first sure that the wind had already dealt some blow of substance, that something had come loose, the cabin's felt roof-cloth maybe. But when he made his way around the starboard flank, he could see no obvious damage.

The three crewmen were standing around, staring down through the box-hole into the hold. He moved beside them, thinking that maybe they had snagged something odd in the catch, a seal maybe or a small shark. Judging from Lavery's shout, something that could stir up a heap of trouble for them. Lavery was the eldest of the crewmen, somewhere in his forties, short and heavy set, with a large head pushed down between brick shoulders and a cap of clipped white hair over a tight face and small blue eyes.

'What's the idea of slacking?' Finnegan growled, but not in an ill-tempered way. 'We got ourselves a hell of a blow coming down on us.'

Lavery didn't pull his eyes from the hold, but the two younger men looked up at Finnegan. Browne stood nearest. He was a man stuck somewhere in his twenties, a hard worker who even in drunkenness didn't rate as much of a talker. There was a hard fold around his mouth that made Finnegan sure that he was going to offer some words now but the look passed and nothing came.

The third crewman was the youngest on board. Still the boy side of sixteen, overgrown for deck work and with the narrow droop of a flower. He was Luke, and he had been with Finnegan only since summer. It was still heads or tails whether he would make the grade but he had the attitude at least, if not yet the build, and he did what he was told without complaint. He was also boy enough to still be quick with a joke, and though none of the others smiled except when the jokes turned particularly crude, it was clear enough to a sea captain that everyone better than just put up with him.

It was left to Luke to speak. He did so with a nod of his drooping head. 'In there, Skip.'

Lavery stepped enough aside for Finnegan to see. At first he could make out nothing much, just darkness specked with the silver flashes of mackerel. He was about to ask just what he was supposed to be looking at exactly when, through the mound of fish, he noticed the hand. He started, and Browne nodded, as if in confirmation.

'Jesus Christ,' he whispered, straightening up and looking around stupidly at his men. 'What's going on here?'

'What do we do, Jack?' Lavery asked. He had been with

Finnegan more than twenty years, time enough that there was nothing between them where names were concerned.

Somehow, the twilight had slipped down further towards darkness; its stealth was shocking. Out across the ocean now there was nothing at all to see but for the slow bruised trawl of the distant lighthouse's yellow cast. The storm was busy holding itself down, but they all knew that it would soon enough break free.

Finnegan tried to think. He'd have to call the police, that was a given. But the storm complicated things. It was an hour away, if that, and then it would have the boat thrashing about and maybe smashed against the pier if they didn't get it tethered down. He nodded to himself.

'All right,' he said, and he was glad to hear that his voice was steady. The others were frightened, and it wouldn't do to let them see that he was frightened too. 'One chance.' He glanced around at each man in turn. 'Anyone want to tell me anything?'

They all shook their heads no, and he believed them.

'Anyone know who it is?'

Again they all shook their heads, though the body was still buried beneath the pile of herring, and no one could yet rightly answer such a question. An ache worked through him sharply; that was the whole day's catch all gone to hell. But it couldn't be helped.

'We've lost ourselves a day's work,' Lavery said, his voice a low rumble, the grit of a lifetime breathing of the sea. He'd just had the thought, and spoken.

'Luke,' Finnegan said, ignoring other talk. 'You'll have to go ashore and call the guards. Tell 'em what we found and tell 'em the situation, about the storm and all. The rest of us will try to tie her fast, keep her fixed good enough so that they'll be able to at least take a look at things when they come.'

Luke was gazing down into the dark hold. 'Maybe it was just someone we snagged in the nets.' But everyone knew that they would have noticed such a thing on the trawl.

'Either way, the guards will want to know it,' Finnegan said. 'So get going.'

The boy nodded, and began to clamber awkwardly up the crude water-greened steps of the pier's wooden docking ladder. The others watched him slowly rise up into the growing darkness.

'What a mess,' Lavery muttered. 'Christ, we're all for it now.'

Browne looked up, the ropes set for lashing busy in his hand. 'What do you mean, Lav?'

Lavery shrugged, spoke his answer as much to Finnegan as to Browne: 'Well, think about it. The guards show up here, they'll be pointing the finger at one or all of us. Even if they can't pin us with the stiff, they'll have some bullshit thing, interfering with the scene of a crime or something like that.' He let his face turn from one to the other, and then raised his eyes to include the unmistakable silhouette of Luke, standing above them on the pier but frozen from his mission. Lavery's voice was calm, as if he were explaining a particular rope knot to a novice, and his expression was serious but undisturbed. At last he shrugged again, muttered, 'I'm just saying,' and stooped to the task of roping the boat.

The others didn't move. Caught in a paralysis, their minds raced to make some sense of all this. Only the worst possibilities pushed to the fore. Finnegan gestured for Luke to come back down. 'This is a problem that bears some thinking about,' he said.

The wind was already rising and the *Bella Vista* leaned its starboard side heavily skyward into the thickened swell. But Lavery had made much progress with the ropes, and beyond the fine salt bullets of spray and the heaving movement, they felt relatively secure.

'So what can we do?' asked Browne, more animated than anyone could remember. 'Just hold fast till morning?'

By way of answer, Lavery began to lay out the facts: 'As I see it, we call in the guards now, they'll cut this boat open. Unless we got ourselves a talking body down there, they'll take whatever scraps of evidence they find. And what'll that be but fingerprints, maybe the odd thread of clothes. I'd lay my cut of a week's haul that most of that'll point to one or all of us. See what I'm saying?'

Finnegan didn't like it, but he nodded, because Lavery was right. 'Yeah, and don't forget, we're out-of-towners here. I think it's fairly safe to assume that we rode around the last two days and nights with our friend below as company. That means we carried a stowaway all the way from home. And face it; we know pretty much everyone that would have any business around our own small docks, right? If it turns out that any or all of us should know this poor bastard, well ...'

The thing left unsaid spoke loudest of all.

'And they'll be keen to know how we had failed to notice a stiff in the basement for two whole days on a boat of this size.' Lavery scratched his chin. He still showed an outer calm, the white pins of his hair plastered down across his spray-soaked brow, but Finnegan had to wonder whether such words of persuasion were born of logic or of cunning. He hated to think the thing that he was thinking about the most trusted of his crew, the man he regarded as his closest confidant, but it was there, large in his mind, and he couldn't help it.

'No,' Luke said, loud with obvious fear. 'I know why we didn't see it. The tarp, it must have been covering it but then shifted with the weight of the haul.'

Browne nodded in agreement. 'And probably the sea too. We hit pretty rough water last night.'

'Still doesn't change anything, though,' Lavery muttered. 'The police come, they'll be looking at us for the fix.'

It began to rain. The plan, before the body had come to light, was to unload the herring, set the boat a distance out and drop an anchor bow and stern. Let the wind and the waves turn her all they wanted. For the crew it was the usual schedule: go ashore, get drunk and sleep in a nice warm bed in one of the cheap motels along the front. Now it was too late for all of those things. The boat had been lashed securely to the pier. They could still go ashore now but they wouldn't, not with this matter left unresolved. The rain came in sheets, heavier than the spray but not by much. It pummelled the deck and slashed dully at their oilcloths. Without a word, Finnegan turned and went below, and one by one the others followed, Lavery, last, dropping the door on the hold.

Below, they squeezed around a small wooden table bolted in place. Finnegan had produced a plain green bottle already a few fingers shy of full, and he splashed cheap whiskey into four discoloured coffee mugs. For a stretch of time that seemed forever, the men sipped the raw spirits and tried with varying degrees of success to come to terms with the situation at hand.

Lavery began, speaking directly to Finnegan. 'So, what are our options?'

It was less a question than a prompt, or an excuse to take the floor.

Finnegan tossed a hand in a gesture to continue.

Lavery nodded. 'All right,' he said, his voice raised an unnecessary notch now for the benefit of everyone. 'The way I see it, we have two choices. One, we can send Luke for the law. They'll come and take us in, question us about what we know, probably impound the *Bella Vista* as evidence so that even if they turn us loose our fishing days are done and dusted for the foreseeable future. And that's *if* they turn us loose. More likely they'll keep us hanging, because our prints must be all over this scene and barring lucky miracles that's all they're really going to have. Then, like Jack here already said, if they can find some kind of a link between us and the stiff, well, this case is looking suddenly more and more solid for a fit up.' He turned his head slowly in a full half circle, meeting the eyes of each man in turn.

'That's the first option. But we have a second, though it won't sound great to you boys, not at first anyway. The second option is, we forget that we ever saw anything down in that hole. We've got probably an hour or so left before the worst of this storm hits. We could go back up on deck and try to get as much of our catch as we can on ice and maybe save something from the day. Then when we go out tomorrow to tackle the sound, well, we dump out all that we lost, everything that remains down in that hold.'

Finnegan was waiting for him to throw off another shrug and mutter, 'I'm just saying,' but he didn't. Instead he met each man's face in turn again, starting with Finnegan on his left and ending with Luke directly across the table from him, and said, 'I kind of like the second option myself, but I'll go along with whatever decision you fellas make.'

'I think we should go to the police,' Browne said, in a voice so low that it barely carried over the muted roar of the coming storm. He looked only at his hands with their criss-crossed mesh of white ridged scars. 'All of that stuff is circumstantial. We have nothing to hide. I say we take our chances.'

After that there was a long silence as every man examined his own conscience. Finnegan listened to the wind and felt the waves thickening against the boat's hull. He filled the cups again with whiskey and they drank.

Luke lowered his mug and cleared his throat, and it was clear to everyone that he would have the deciding vote in the matter; Finnegan wouldn't go against the majority of his crew. Like Browne, the boy didn't raise his eyes. 'I go with Lav,' he muttered. Then he did look up, but only at Browne. 'Say they put a fix on it. We'd be finished. We should go out tomorrow and forget any of this ever happened.'

There was no answer to that. Finally Finnegan stood; balance on a heaving boat was no problem for one who had spent so much of his life at sea. He climbed the steps and disappeared. The others just sat there, listening to his heavy boots slowly crawl the length of the boat overhead.

Lavery knew what he was talking about, but he had been wrong about one thing; they didn't have an hour before the worst of the storm hit. Up on deck it was already here. Wind swept across the boat, each gust weighted with bullets of rain. Finnegan's heavy yellow oilskin slicker ballooned around him as he fought out an advance, and there was a moment when he really feared being swept overboard. In that black sea he wouldn't last a minute. He hunched low and braced himself against the starboard onslaught, grasping for handholds of support wherever they offered themselves and trying to judge the moment when the wind shifted or each whipping gust abated and he could surge a step ahead. The ten feet to the hold seemed a mile away across no man's land. But he made it, dropped to his knees and struggled to pull open the drop door. Then he lowered himself down into the pile of slowly rotting fish, flailed in the absolute darkness to find the light-switch and felt the first bloom of real terror rupture in his chest when his hand found nothing but the flaking slats of the limewashed walls.

He stopped, wrestled his breath steady and let a forced calm overcome the worst of the fear. It helped. Slowly he reached out for the walls and gently began to trail his fingers back and forth in a sweeping motion until they settled upon the grease-smothered muslin cloth used as waterproof cladding for the light switch. In an instant the hold exploded with light. Piles of fish shone, dead eyes gaping.

The hand had been lost again; the shift of the boat had concealed it once more beneath the pliable cargo. They had been just lucky to have seen it at all, Finnegan thought to himself, except lucky was hardly the right word. He knew what he had to do.

Reluctantly, he drew deep of the rancid air and began to dig, gagging with the stench and with thoughts of what he might find.

What he found was not the hand but a bare calf. With nothing now pumping through him but repulsion, he burrowed into the clammy stumps of herring and through the pile rose an ankle and a bare foot.

It was a woman. The calf and shin bone were more or less shaved clean and the small stubby toe nails showed the clear remains of flaking black nail varnish. Finnegan pulled away into a corner of the hold and began to vomit. He expelled little of substance and the recently consumed whiskey tore at his throat and flushed sour in his mouth, but he felt better for it. 'Take it easy,' he gasped to himself, reaching out with one hand for the support of the wall, but no part of him listened. He just wanted to get this thing done and to get out of there, back down into the cabin, back to the whiskey. He made for a higher point in the pile of fish, judging by the position of the foot roughly where the head should be, and he didn't have to dig long before his hands felt the wiry scrub of hair. He lifted the body, head and shoulders, to the surface.

Her eyes were open but fixed on nothing, and in the harsh overhead light her flesh had the greyish-blue tinge of decay. It was a terrible thing to see, but hypnotic too. He stared at that face, awaiting the glimmer of recognition to spark in his mind, but the mask of death made it a long time in coming. Then, in a way as sudden as the urge to vomit had been, some veil slipped and he knew her.

'Maggie,' he whispered, the name scraping from his trembling mouth. Just Maggie; no surname that he had ever heard. She did business down along the docks, a wretched creature for as long as he had known her, a length of time that must have been going on for surely twenty years. A prostitute, reduced by age and alcohol and God only knew what kind of drugs to the very lowest rung of society's ladder. It hadn't always been so, but for a long time she had played the wretch, her hard, thin body stooped, her hatchet face far removed from her actual mid- to late-thirties age. Earning a crust from the fishermen staggering back to their boats after a night of hard drinking, and the cold back-seat dawns with the sick businessmen on their way to the city and a life far removed from the one she lived. Sometimes from the boat, she could be heard laughing as if in joy, but it was a cold sound, unsettling. Like an asylum shriek. It always made him want to turn away.

Looking down into that contorted crone's face now, it was hard to imagine a time when it had flexed kindly with youth, or that she had ever known any kind of beauty. But she had, if only the desperate sort that leads to no good things. Tawny middle-length hair fell lankly from her head and one black strap of a cheap dress cut into the bowed collarbone inside her narrow shoulder. The other strap hung loose and broken, and the dress sagged in a way that exposed most of the fleshy sweep of one small breast. Finnegan didn't want to touch her, though as a younger man he, like so many others, had paid his pittance over to her for that small pleasure more than once.

The urge to run welled up inside him, but he hated the idea of letting her lie there all alone in the blackness with the herring, and he steadied his footing and lifted her free. Cradled in his arms her weight was negligible, a thing that seemed most tragic of all. Her head rolled over the crook of his arm, and he tried not to see her death in his mind.

There was no way that he could see to lift her out on deck so he settled for laying her in a corner of the hold. Then he peeled off his rain slicker and spread it down over her face and upper body, and without further thought, hauled himself out through the trapdoor and back into the sweep of the storm once again.

In the cabin, no one had moved. They looked up when Finnegan returned, soaked to the bone without his oilskin coat, and watched as he eased back into his seat, poured himself a whiskey from the bottle and drank it off in one long, unsteady swallow. Then he poured himself a second and lingered over it.

Browne cleared his throat, thought to say something but instead just shrugged and kept his silence.

'It was a woman,' Finnegan said, voice a husk with the whiskey. He looked into his mug. 'Maggie.'

'Maggie?' Browne said. 'Not Maggie from back …'

'Yeah.'

After that they worked through the bottle and on into a second, not in the rabid way of usual but just to fill a void. Outside, the music of the storm was an ever-present. Finnegan parted with details almost grudgingly, offering only fragments at a time. Somewhere into the second bottle, Lavery, with enough facts to hand, lay out his thoughts as to how it must have happened, how some customer, either by accident or in anger, had broken her neck. Probably right there on the dockside. The *Bella Vista*'s hold was a dark place, better than the water because maybe she'd float there and be seen. Or maybe the whole thing was blind panic and the *Bella* had just been unluckily convenient.

Near dawn they had all consumed enough whiskey to sleep, but Finnegan didn't want the dreams that he knew were waiting, and instead he left them and went up on deck to watch for light. The storm had mostly blown itself out over the past hours and the wind had fallen away to just a strong breeze. The sea still held a swollen shape that continued to rock the boat even with the secure bindings of the ropes, and rain fell but as a light drizzle. He moved to the bow, the furthest point from the hold, and gazed off into the darkness. Sometimes the touch of the lighthouse's crawling beam fixed itself out across the water but mostly the night's cover held. It was cold and wet without his coat, but it let him feel alive, and that was what he needed most.

He didn't turn when he heard the footsteps crossing the deck.

'Luke,' he muttered in acknowledgement. On a boat, you quickly learned to identify people by their step.

'Skip,' Luke said, and moved to stand alongside. 'Storm's blown.'

'I reckon.'

'We pulling out soon?'

Finnegan nodded. 'Couple of hours. Let 'em sleep a while.' In the darkness, Luke looked pale and very young. His droop was pronounced by the cold and his long mouth was pinched into a slit. His big eyes were filled with faraway things. 'Why aren't you catching a few z's yourself?'

'Wasn't feeling all that tired.' Finnegan knew that it was because he was thinking about the dead woman in the hold.

This was a time that most of the boats should be setting out, but the bay was quiet. Probably, the men of the other boats had steeled themselves against the storm and were still sleeping off the effects, propped up against a bar or in some bed paid for by the hour.

'Are we going with Lav's idea about dropping the body in the Sound?' The boy's voice was straining for casual but Finnegan felt something stir in his mind, an alarm bell signalling something not quite right.

He didn't turn from the ocean and kept his own words steady. 'You mean Maggie?'

'Yeah.' Whispered in a small voice.

Finnegan rolled his shoulders. 'I suppose it's best,' he conceded, 'even though it doesn't feel right.' Now he glanced at Luke. Silence was no friend to the boy, and suddenly he was certain. 'I'm still not decided. Maybe calling in the law would be best.' It was like baiting a hook, and just sitting back to wait for the desperation of the pull.

Luke fought it, but to no avail. 'What about what we were saying, about the fingerprints and the fit up and all of that? And you've been down there yourself now, so you'll be all over the scene.'

'Still not much to go on,' Finnegan said. 'Not really. It's my boat, after all. No court would nod to that.'

'Yeah, but don't forget. Even if they believe us, they'll impound the boat as evidence, won't they?' All pretence of calm was abandoned now. 'Lav's right. The Sound's the easiest way, for all of us.'

The silence after the outburst felt like a judgement, and Finnegan let it spin out, then asked, 'Why, Luke? Why did you kill her?'

Luke stood trembling and if there was one final consideration of denial then it quickly passed. He broke, fell to his knees and, with his face cupped in his large red hands, began to cry. Finnegan stood there, looking down at the bow of head and shoulders and the arched back now jerked with the heaves of long-held anguish tearing loose. He offered no touch of comfort, just waited for the tears to pass and for his question to be answered. He had seen and done a lot of things himself, not all of them paid for. Wasn't that how it was for everyone? But he couldn't find it in him to feel sympathy, not for something like this. So, he stood and waited, and when enough time had passed the worst of Luke's hysterics eased.

'It was an accident. I swear it was.' Pleading eyes scoured his captain's face for some kind of mercy. What he found there was enough to continue. He bowed his head and his words came in wet whispers, staccato stabs on tremulous breath. 'I was coming back to the boat and she was just there. She tried me, you know, laughing and saying that I must be a big boy to be out so late. I'd been drinking and I guess I was drunk, and her offer sounded good.'

He broke off to support himself against a shuddering wave. His mouth twisted in a gesture of loathing. Finnegan wondered if the loathing was for Maggie and what she was or for himself and what he had done. A safe guess would be a little of both.

'I was curious, you know, about what it was like. And it was pretty dark down there, so I didn't have to see too much. But then she started to scream that I was hurting her, that I didn't have to play so rough, and I guess I hit her, just to shut her up. I swear I never meant to ...'

Still on his knees he hunched down and began to cry again, not with the same intensity as before, just the soft tears of fear tempered with a certain relief of a weight lifted.

Finnegan turned his eyes to ocean again. The drizzle had eased. Far to the east a pale white slash cut water loose from sky, though for a time to come yet they would continue to share a deep slate colour. After the storm the heavy swell still roiled, but for Finnegan at least it offered a sense of calm, the welcome isolation. Out there, the whole world was reduced to a length of twenty-four feet, a world he governed in a manner right or wrong. Even now, lashed to a pier, his word still ruled. Something eased within; he had made up his mind.

'Get up, boy.'

Luke moved slowly upright but remained on his knees. Even then, man and boy were almost of a height.

'Get up I said. We have work to do if we want to make the Sound at a decent hour.' He spat overboard and began to move around the pier side of the boat, but he stopped with the sound of the small child's voice rising behind him. He didn't turn back, just stood.

'So you're not going to the guards?'

'No.'

'Thanks.'

Finnegan just grunted. It was a nothing sound, certainly not an acknowledgement. 'This is my boat and I am responsible for my crew. We'll go out to the Sound and, like Lavery says, we'll empty the hold. Damned waste.'

The ache of tears was choking Luke. 'I won't let you down again, Skip.'

'You're right about that. We should be back to port in three days. Maybe while ashore you'll decide that fishing's not really your thing.' He paused to let there be no misunderstanding as to the intent of his words. Then he grunted again, a scratched sound, basted in hard, sardonic laughter. 'Funny, my money would have been on Lavery or Browne. Never you. Not in a million years. Damned waste.'

Then, leaving the boy alone on the helm, he moved away to the part of the boat that was still wrapped in darkness and began releasing the binding ropes from the pier's stanchion poles in anticipation of the day.

TOURIST SEASON

In recent years, tourists have begun to discover the island, drawn by the glossy postcard images of misty summer dawns, quaint villages and the brilliant sunsets that burnish the placid waters of Gull's Cove, drawn too by the notion of a land still pretending to exist outside the passage of time. Occasionally they stop us to ask for directions, and they are always well-mannered, their voices full of rolling Dublin brashness or clipped Germanic precision. The men sport the first dustings of a holiday beard and for some reason always look older than the women, and the women are usually blonde and manage to look pretty even when decked out in a designer raincoat or poncho. Women who like to be prepared. And we smile and make a play out of telling them the places they should be seeking out, our island's best kept secrets. The island is small, roughly as long as it is wide, maybe three and a half miles from water to water, so we understand that it is less the directions they want than the opportunity to converse, however briefly, with a local.

Tourism has become important, even critical, to our survival. It is our bread and butter, now that the fishing industry is all but finished.

At night, in Costigan's, we settle into our well-worn

places at the bar and start in on the serious business of drinking, and now and again we mutter in Irish amongst ourselves, not really for privacy's sake, though that is sometimes a consideration, but because it is our language still, though it is on the wane. When the tourists push through the door we look up, nod a welcome and then quickly look away, and after just the slightest hesitation they gravitate towards one another, strangers made to share the bond of foreignness. French couples sit with Americans, people from Cork chat with people from London, but until the music starts they must feel exiled there in the corner snug or at the tables and low stools in the middle of the floor, and they compensate by talking a little too loud, or maybe it is just the way that people used to grappling with the noises of a city have learned to talk. Their voices punch through the rumble of the barroom, intent on swapping details with their newest best friends of places they visited today, or yesterday, places like the shale beach out at Tully's Point or the truly stunning views to be had from the picnic spot up at Crom's Well.

Then the music starts, and it is we who are exiled. Mulgrew and his spinster daughters huddle in the corner and play jigs and slip-reels that have never been written down, tunes that have been passed along through generations of players and which have made it from our shores only as far as the wind can carry them. A bodhrán keeps time for a fiddle and a tin whistle, the instruments worked by hands and fingers worn to stone but made so skilled by years of nights spent at the fireside. Loneliness simmers in the racing notes as the fiddle leans out of its jig and goes screaming away on a few minutes of lament, but it is theatrical, a hollow nod to bygone times.

And afterwards, the cap is passed around, the navy corduroy made damp from old Mulgrew's exertions, the two or three hours with his neck bent to the fiddle, and we dig for the loose change weighing down our pockets. The few coins that we can spare lie scattershot above the tourist offerings, the Euro notes, fives and even tens, money earned in ways that can be more casually spent. Tonight's music was meant for them, and they are happy to pay for the privilege.

The old man, Mulgrew, and his middle-aged daughters Áine and Cait, might be nothing more than colour now, a limited element of the ambience, but at least they have found a place for themselves in the changing ways of the island. By playing what the tourists want to hear, they can live more or less as they have always lived, playing their music and, when the hour grows late and quiet enough, singing the old songs, the drifting narratives tragic in word, desolate in melody.

It is different for me. Over the past decade or so, the fishing industry has collapsed, and yet it remains a way of life for those of us who can do nothing else. The tourists enjoy lingering down around the waterfront, middle-aged couples in their knee-length trousers and with their yellow slickers billowing out around them in the breeze, holding hands to support one another as they pick their way carefully out along the short pier, the greenish algae-smeared timbers giving a treacherous edge to the idea of casual strolling. They watch us in our boats, not knowing that our lives now are just shadows of what they had once been, before the Spanish trawlers that come up from the Mediterranean and raked clean the ocean bottom, over-fishing along the limit lines of International Waters. They see us as they see Mulgrew, not understanding what we have lost.

I want the island as it was in my grandfather's time, or my father's, or the way it was back when I was just a child. These days the yachts come and go, just as they always have, eighteen- or twenty-eight-foot slabs that boast of wealth beyond compare but offer no real connection at all to the sea. Those on board wear linen shirts and dark glasses, never anything of necessity, and they drink champagne and look too beautiful to be inhabiting our corner of the world. When I was a child we'd stare at them with awe, and I suppose that is no less so today.

Reliable skiffs still mottle the harbour, but I'll forever hold fond memories of how our lives revolved around the small timber currach boats, those oar-driven vessels with open bellies and flaking waterproof paintwork that for generations had served us so faithfully. There are still a few of us on the island who make our living from the sea, but we know that our days are numbered. The time is drawing close when it will become a thing of the past to row out with the dawn still only hinting at the horizon, rowing an hour or more out to settle over the places handed down to us through hundreds of years of lessons learned in hard and tragic ways and casting our nets for the mackerel that still come, or for the herring that come less and less now. A few of us continue to persevere, but it feels like fighting the tide, and month on month our numbers lessen as the others, mostly those with families, bow to the inevitable. We know the sea, as much as anyone can ever really know it, and though we could probably make a decent enough living, in the summertime anyway, at offering pleasure cruises, island tours or angling excursions, for those of us who refuse to bend such things would feel a little too much like play. We fight a big war, but yield to so many skirmishes.

Sometimes of an evening, when I'm either sitting in my boat or crouched and busy at trying to mend the snags and tears in my nets as they lay stretched out on the pier, I'm aware of the tourists who like to photograph things. They come down just as night is threatening to close in because the air feels thick and other-worldly then and even though they understand nothing of the island's ways they can feel the strangeness that is real and unreal at the same time. If the sky is clear and it is late summer the sun will lie down on the far edge of the water as a bloody western mess and spill itself out in a way that makes for just the most spectacular image an eye can ever hope to behold. But even if, as is more likely, the hour is banked in cloud, the glow of last daylight is still a thing worth seeing.

The tourists come with their cameras and open their shutters, and I crouch, fastening my nets for tomorrow's shoals, and listen to them as they snap away. It is always the same, the gradual awareness that they have taken their fill of landscape pictures and are now training their camera's lens on me. I know I must look a sight, but that is what they want, the idea of a man stooped low over his work well into the last half-lit hour, milking the day of its worth as his grizzled hands toil at binding together his ravaged nets. To them, I am a glimpse of another time, in the same way as Mulgrew and his spinster daughters are, and for the sake of art we can all ignore the fact that they are seeing what they want to see. None of them have ever asked for permission to take my photograph, though I believe that is less out of disrespect or poor manners than that they simply don't want to disturb me in my work. Maybe they think that I won't understand, but I do. Posing without meaning to, raising the nets just a little so that they can better catch my profile and so that the ropes of kelp spill some way free of their bunching, my small effort at making the picture feel a little more alive, I often wonder just how many living room walls or mantelpieces around the world carry a framed image of my face. Even as outdated as we have become, as ill-fitting with our present surround, men like me have our uses, it seems.

The work is just as tough now as it was when I was a boy and starting out, learning the ways from my father. It is all a matter of perspective. Yes, the fish are less in number, but they are still there and I still take enough to make a living, if a frugal one. With so few of us out now, competition is not really much of an issue anymore. The restaurants on the island, Dorney's over in Missal Bay and the Frenchman's place, Michel's, here in Gull's Cove, need fresh fish to meet the demand. The guesthouses want some too, those that offer evening meals. We have worked out an arrangement that allows us all to get by, though the winters can be lean and when storms come we all suffer.

Nobody lives a life completely free of regret. The trick, I have often heard it said, is how you cope with the situations that let you down. The worst mistakes, I now believe, are the things left to go unsaid, or undone.

I am the last of my people here on the island. I have a sister in Dublin but she has long since cut ties with this place, and when my time finally comes the line will stop with me, since I have never married. Such knowledge weighs heavily on a man as he steps into middle age. The tourists sometimes trail young children after them but more usually they appear as couples, and there is something about how comfortable they seem, how intently they share everything, that makes it difficult not to wonder what else the wider world has to offer. All around, there are reminders for me of what my life could have been, but it is the first glimpse of the tourists that really brings the message home. The details of how they look at one another can seem slight but never inconsequential, and the unwavering love between them is as trusting to nature as the freefall sweep of the gulls at feeding time or the flashes of shale that crawl out into the sea from the headland. Watching these couples walking hand in hand, so delightful in their imperfections, forces me to remember Gráinne all over again.

Two nights ago in Costigan's the stout had tasted just right to a throat parched to bone by the long shift at sea, and when I had consumed enough to start losing control I got up from the bar and went to sit a while with Flor Howlett. He is usually to be found at the table nearest the door, alone with a single drop of Jameson set carefully on the table before him, and throughout the long evenings he does no more than lean in to breathe of its fumes, his mind counting the hours until closing time and anticipating the pleasure of how, at the last bell, he'll take the whiskey down in a single hard swallow. 'I like to save it for the road home,' he explains, the countless times that the question has been asked. 'Jameson's as decent company as a man of my age will likely find.'

He is old now, and well known on the island for his miserly ways. He says he favours this particular brand of whiskey because of its harshness to the tongue, but we all know that it is because Jameson is the cheapest brand that Costigan stocks.

Though twice my age, he recognises me as a kindred spirit. Back in his better days he was known as a masterful hand with the thatch, and he travelled far in the company of his brothers while there was still a shilling's profit to be turned in constructing a well-laid roof, back before slate made everyone too good for the crafted bedding of straw and knitted reed. He has a place a half mile or so outside the village, behind and above the cove, a small rundown cottage that fringes the roadside just where the land peaks above the western inlet. His thatching days are long since done, and his own roof, pummelled thin by years of rain and sea gales and dipping in a critical state, is good for little more now than nesting rats. Since Gráinne's departure, neatness has lost whatever importance it may once have had, and he claims in a voice everyone believes that the rats don't bother him at all.

'How's the fishing, young Finn?' he asked, and I could only shrug.

'Dead in the water, Florrie.'

He leaned over his glass and filled his lungs. 'Like the thatch, so.' I am allowed to sit with him only because he knows that I will buy him drink. I did what was expected of me, telling him to drink up, and calling with a nod to Costigan behind the counter. Costigan unfolded his thick forearms and pulled a tot from the upturned bottle on the wall, but Howlett has a routine fixed by years of practice and he drank the first whiskey only when he had the full assurance of the second sitting safely before him.

Gráinne is our obvious connection, or rather the loss of her from our lives, and in our sober moments I am sure that we each spend part of the day holding the other accountable in some way for that. It is always easier to blame someone else for our own mistakes. But drunk, or at least in the environs of drink, such blame matters less than the sharing of pain. An hour or so of casual companionship shapes what words cannot.

Our conversation had a drab familiarity, spare efforts at throwing up subjects of no real consequence. Between talk, we listened to Mulgrew fiddling a variation of O'Carolan, some melody that fit well enough above the incessant background chatter of the tourists. Their snapping accents seemed rich with curiosity when set against the guttural snarls of our own words. At some point in the night, I found a way of asking after Gráinne. 'Have you heard from herself at all recently?' Something like that, said casually, as I sat with my arm outstretched along the back of the snug's three-cornered carpet seating, and I averted my stare, feigning some interest perhaps in the music or in a face across the bar.

I never like to use her name much, and I don't suppose he likes hearing it. We both knew exactly who I meant.

'A letter came,' he said, his tone careful but well enough mannered, probably in the hopes of more whiskey. 'A week back, I'd say it must be. The usual kind of thing. Everything's grand. The twins made their Confirmation, and Jim, that's the husband, is after getting a bump up the ladder. He's deputy head of something or other now.'

There was nothing left for me to do but swallow deeply from my pint. I know Jim is the husband, and I know that his good job in the bank has been able to provide her with a decent home and nice things. But I can do without hearing it again, even if I am fool enough to ask for it. The curve of the glass pulled my mouth into a clownish smile, and it held there of its own accord, mocking me, as I pretended to digest the news.

'She says she's content now,' he added, a final nail for the coffin, after we had listened while the tune played itself out. Across the bar, Mulgrew scratched his cheek with the heel of the bow and then for good measure pulled a scream from the fiddle strings. One of his daughters, Cait, leaned in and offered a suggestion, and off they went again, not counting it in, not agreeing on a key, just playing, in perfect synch with one another. When they are lost in the music nothing else matters to them.

If Gráinne had stayed, and if I had been a better sort of man, she'd be sharing my home now and not some banker's, and if there had to be children then they would be my children, speaking with my accent. I'd still be fishing, I suppose, and it would be difficult for us to make ends meet on the little that I earn, but one thing would be different: I'd be happy. I am convinced that she knew how I felt about her, but she could only wait so long for something that I didn't know how to say. I realise that she's better off where she is, but I'm not better off without her.

What we had together, the lovely year that closed out our late teens, might seem slight when put down as words. It was a lifetime ago, and at nineteen errors in judgement are allowed, even expected, so maybe we were both just unlucky to stumble across our big moment at what was surely too young an age. Or maybe I knew what we had but was too headstrong or too afraid to take the chance. No particular detail from that time carries any greater importance for me than the next, but I think upon that year now as my golden time because it still shines so brightly in my mind. A long-ago year that has reduced all the rest to a sort of half life. I can't imagine how Gráinne must look now but I can still see her as she was back then. Even the smallest detail of her face is only a thought's distance away, and a thousand early mornings have found me out in the boat, alone and with nothing in any direction for the eye to see but the torpid heave of waves, when it has been nearly possible to believe that she is there with me. The past can exist as a ghost; I have learned that much with certainty. We are haunted by our very worst mistakes, and sometimes the wind across the water sounds just like the murmur of her laughter.

Flor Howlett's features have all the softness of a wild clawing briar, but as gentle as Gráinne was she had the same eyes, the murky green of shaded grass, and the very same way of pinching her mouth when she considered a problem. His opposite in every way I could ever imagine, yet she was undeniably her father's daughter. When Costigan's closed I walked up the hill with him, feeling some need to see him home safely. It was an unnecessary gesture, of course; he is well used to the road and the darkness and could well have done without my company because, even feeble as he has become, there is no place for him to fall that threatens any more harm than that treacherous, rat-infested cottage.

'Will you come in for a few minutes?' he said, when we reached the gap where a rusted iron gate had hung for years beyond count before simply disappearing, but I glanced at the cottage's sunken roof and the small windows thick with the crud of years' accumulated dust, salted wind and long abandoned meshes of cobweb, and I shook my head.

'I won't, Flor. The Brill are in and I'll have to get the boat out early. Thanks all the same, though.'

The way he tilted his head told me that he knew what I wanted to ask: Whether or not she ever mentions me at all in her letters. But I didn't even try to find the words because I was afraid of what the answer might have been, and something kept him from speaking it anyway, some fear of his own.

'Well,' said Howlett. 'Goodnight, so.'

I waited until he went inside before turning and making my way back down the hill. The breeze that started up carried a sound that might have been the rats wailing themselves awake in the thatch, rousing with the intent of a night spent foraging, or might have been nothing at all but the voice of the wind. On the island, every element has a tale to tell, and the wind no less than the water.

My unasked question lingered, and I shifted it in my mind as I followed the road down, all the while telling myself that I was better off not knowing one way or the other. I suppose that's right. Some will say that it does no good to mire ourselves completely in times gone by, but I say it does no great harm either. What it comes down to is acceptance. I have seen and done enough to know that I had my chance, and there is only room for that sort of chance once in a lifetime. Settling might bring a certain amount of joy, and there are plenty who have made good out of second-best or even less, but that is not for everyone, and I don't think it is for me.

I will turn forty in October. I have been fishing from boats since I was six years old, taught by my father how to read the water for signs and also the proper way to cast and haul and how to ride the waves when the swell thickens. That I never learned to swim a single stroke is the way it should be, according to our island ways, and I have never questioned the logic of it, only accepted. Overboard means the end to everything, and there is a peculiar sort of comfort in such an assurance.

What makes reaching forty so difficult for a man like me is that I know I am too old now to change, and I am being left behind as the world, even the island, moves ahead into a new age.

The coming of summer reminds me of my loneliness, April leading into May, and the first arrival of the tourists. Winter is better, because there are no distractions, only the enduring worry of rough seas and strong Atlantic winds, only the danger of slipped concentration or the side-on freak assault of a tumbling wave. The fish have become scarce, but I never worry too much about that. Even when the icy shards of sleet gives the day a suicidal edge I take my chances, squinting my eyes and steering my boat out of the cove, wading through the pale ochre swaths of foam that crawl outward from the timber breakers and on out into the churning sea, out to where the land, even the island, becomes little more than myth. Thinking of what might have been, I find a place to fish and cast my nets.

PUT DOWN

By first morning the wind gloated in its vigour. McCarthy filled the doorway, his big shoulder pressed against the jamb. The sky, even with the dawn, was black and up here the air snapped cold threat. He scratched his sunken cheek for the three days of beard to bristle dryly. There'd be no storm, thank God, but that wind was still enough to keep him landed. The door jamb had his weight and he slumped against it, giving up, in no hurry now for anything.

Somewhere behind him in the darkened cottage, Bríd worked noisily at her kitchen chores, her irritation as volatile as this February weather. Soon he'd catch the hiss of the bacon in the pan, the spit of the lard. Already she had collected the morning's yield of eggs from the small hen house. He knew that she'd be thinking of the money lost but the seethe of her anger came from a place deeper within, an anger made of the conspiracies of all the things wrong with her life.

McCarthy studied the sky and tried not to think about her yet, and down from the village the bilge of ocean roared explosions against the shoreline's creep of shale. He watched the road for the first inevitable approach of Dinny Shea, that small lope pulling up into the sweep, up from the village to here. But the night's darkness was slow to lift and the road remained empty yet.

His head ached, as much from the lateness in getting to bed as from the few pints down in Harrington's, the pulse ringing sharply behind his eyes. But in the doorway he could breathe, and the day that stretched out before him was a sanctuary now where last night it seemed a hangman's noose. Today there'd be no sea, none of that trauma even for a man who had given up the bulk of the last thirty-four years to its needs. He'd find work in need of doing, but mending nets and knitting lobster heads and scrubbing out the iceboxes and priming the hull and overhauling the motor never felt bad from the safety of the port, never felt like work in the way that starting out cold and tired beneath a heavy dawn into the bloated gape of a winter's sea did.

He stood awhile, content just in the way the bare silhouettes of the roadside sycamore branches tapped out small code rhythms and swayed to the pull of the wind, or how the chorus of the birds rose upwards against the wind in melding, shifting altos, voices wrapping in harmonious virtue. It was good to hear, birdsong an antidote this morning to the sea and the plaintive westerly gale, just as it was always good to see them finally take to flight, sweeping up in torrents from the cloak of trees, black against the slowly lightening sky, free to go wherever they might, in flight bound to nothing but their own craven need to soar.

The kitchen had the cluttered, worn feel of a used place. McCarthy slumped heavily into a chair in the corner. It moaned against his heft but he tipped it back anyway until the chair's front legs and his own booted feet cleared the linoleum long rubbed clean of its pattern and his big shoulders could press supportive against the wall. His left hand clutched one extended leaf of the fold-out table for support, fingers clipping out drum-tap arpeggios.

His mouth was dry. Porter never tasted right in repeat.

The electric light left the morning hollow, stripping it of dimension. It always raised in him a longing for the intimate times of the paraffin lamp.

Bríd loitered at the stove, feeding the pans with the bacon strips. She made no acknowledgement of McCarthy's presence. McCarthy stole glances at her, hoping maybe for a thaw.

In the electric light she looked every bit her age. How her hair hung long and lifeless past her shoulders, giving up the last of its tabby dye colour and letting the dirty ash grey have its way. Her hard face concerned itself with breaking eggs into the pan and cutting slices from a pound of white pudding on the counter. She used to smile once. From her pretty youth, she had grown hawkish. There was nothing pretty about her any more. Her flesh hung in pale ropes, heavily folded with worry lines from her constant cringing and the bones wore that flesh with defiance, protruding from their place like ridges of stone from the softer earth. Her large hooked nose, her cheeks like knuckles beneath the sunken pits of her small jade eyes always staring and always suspicious. And her mouth the judging slash, tight with the repression of things unsaid. You would have to know her well to know her as more than old.

She poured tea into mugs and brought McCarthy's plate to the table. Then she sat across from him and watched him eat.

He ate slowly, not especially hungry. When he was finished he leaned back again to the wall.

'I suppose you'll be staying in today.'

He shrugged.

'Can't be going out in that. The boat would never stand it.'

'Well. There's plenty needs doing around here.'

'There's always plenty needs doing,' he said, his irritation rising.

She let him finish his tea.

He knew that she was holding something back so he took his time, savouring every mouthful. It was what his head needed, hot and sweet. But soon enough it was gone.

'Something the matter?' He felt the wash of weariness. Already the joy of not having to go to sea today had begun to abate.

She fumbled for the right words but it was an act, because this was all rehearsed. 'There's no easy way to say this. It's the dog. You'll have to get rid of him.'

The dog was Buttons, a mongrel fourteen-year-old springer that he had reared from a raw pup.

'Why?'

She shook her head as if saddened by this too.

'He's just more trouble than he's worth. Old as he is, he's good for nothing now but menace. Now he's had after the hens, and that's the last straw. We could far better spend the cost we waste on his feed. Not to mention what he cost us now with them two he killed.'

McCarthy groped for words. This must be what it felt like to be drowning.

'I'll keep him tied up. How about that? Sure he only eats scraps anyway. I won't get rid of him.'

She stood, leaned skeletal across the table. 'He's going, and that's it. You do it or I'll do it myself. Whichever way you like is up to you. But he's going.'

The dog was older even than the children. Lame since an entanglement with a snare some six years back, his left eye stared uselessly milky and his right was sinking down toward that too. He lived by his sense of smell.

But his loyalty could never be questioned. Alert with every dawn, he was always the most intent of the crew, scurrying ahead through the village to the shore, yapping out sharp encouragement, urging the men ever onward. He loved the sea as much as McCarthy despised it, loved how the spray matted his rough hair. In the boat he took up his usual position at the bow, crouched down into the heap of oilcloth. And as Dinny Shea steered them out of the harbour the wind beat the old dog further down into the shelter of the cloth, and he watched the frothing leagues and barked his great joy.

Last night, he got into the hen house. He had been in before, but had in the past been content enough with the chase alone. Last night he killed two of the hens.

It was Peter, the youngest, who had answered the bestial screams. He had to stoop to get inside, and at first there was only a darkness emphasised by the terrified squawks and useless flapping and all the risen specks of dust and hayseed, and through it all the carousing barks of Buttons, throaty and high in the same manner of awaiting a cast stick.

One of the dead hens lay strewn all across the floor, her slight body savaged in what had surely begun as play, but the other lay protectively between the dog's front paws, looking unharmed except for the unnatural stillness. When Peter picked her up, the odd give of her body told him that her neck had been broken.

The back yard, with the shelter of the cottage, was very still. The wind sighed through the thatch, and there was the incessant dance sounds of the rats disturbed. But that wind held no ground back here, and the stillness was somehow worse.

Buttons was in the shed, whining to be set free. Once or twice his paws scratched at the door, urging.

Sometimes when McCarthy laughed his mouth split open and his lips bled in the most painful way. Those times he dragged his tongue slowly across his mouth and the taste was the taste of salt. Blood tasted of salt but the winds of this place tasted of it too. His susceptibility to this particular ailment was just more proof to him that he was not cut out for this kind of life. Sometimes when the weather was especially cold it could take weeks for the chapping to heal, and in those times he would be miserable because it affected the way he ate and even drank. Laughing was the worst thing of all, even smiling, but it was odd how often he felt like smiling, and even laughing, pain be damned, as he watched the dog walking importantly through the village and how he would chase gulls on the pier, not wanting the fish guts that they so savoured at all, but just for the sheer joy of running on a cold morning and of disturbing the peace. The other fishermen would smile too, when they saw Buttons like that.

The hatchet leaned upward from its block bed of wet ash. McCarthy pumped the handle up and down until the blade released itself from the firewood. His big hard fingers took in the coldness of the steel, and he punched the palm of his hand with the blunt backside of the blade. It had a sure heft, and he knew that it was right for what lay ahead.

For just a breath he hesitated at the shed, listening to the dog cry out his excitement and scratch frantically at the door. Paws drummed frenzied circles against the shed floor, hind quarters bounded against the same spot on the wall over and over like something lapping the side of a galvanised drum. Guttural whines rang out, jarring against the hour.

'Whisht,' McCarthy grunted, as the crying became restless barking.

The half-lit morning wore the cloaked aura of impending rain. He knew that he should just open the door and lead Buttons out here into the yard and do it. But he was not ready yet. And not here, for Christ's sake.

Until he was through the back gate that gave onto the fields, Buttons skipped and danced around him, skittish with pent-up energy after the long-incarcerated night. The gate's bottom edge ground hard against the dirt, loose hinges, and the top leaned in full moments before the bottom finally gave way.

Because of what lay ahead, McCarthy felt unnaturally patient, and he stood while Buttons went through the usual motions of sniffing the long grass along the dirt path. Eventually the dog seemed to sense his master's inner turmoil and stopped, muddy haunches set low and trembling, looking up at him. Dark knowing eyes and mouth hanging open, tongue sighing away a throb. Understanding maybe that life was soon to end, or maybe just loyal, as always.

'Come on,' McCarthy said, his words not much more than a drawn-out grunt that a dog could understand, throaty above the trill of every breath.

Obedient, even now this one last time, Buttons led the way out along the path.

White light split the eastern cloud but McCarthy hardly noticed, lost as he was in all the random thoughts of an overtired mind. Memories and aspirations glinted like shards of glass, splinters that carried all their times together. Devastation coloured everything, shadowed the happiness and emphasised the tragic. It was such an ugly thing that he had to do.

The dog furrowed through the long grass at the road's verge, pleased by the coolness of the night's rain. His muzzle when he raised his head again was wet and clotted with mud. He watched McCarthy for the word to stop, that they had come far enough and that they could stop awhile before turning back, he running wild and rolling in the still-green wheat fields, McCarthy settling on a flat part of ditch and tamping his old pipe for a smoke or maybe content just to sit and watch his dog at play. But McCarthy kept a steady pace along the path, up towards the woods.

In the ditches, swathes of cobweb stretched out between ropes of briar, ghostly strands steeled with moisture. From the dyke came the soft slush of running water, shielded by the long grass. Sometimes field gates offered glimpses of the waiting vista: miles of field falling away vaguely north, impeding light cutting to ribbons any lingering dusk.

The hatchet swung idly from his left hand, a promise awaiting conclusion. The woods lay just ahead, another half mile or so, and he hoped to Christ that the darkness up there would make this thing easier.

But then it rose from within, the forceful inflection of Bríd's voice: *Do it now.*

He felt no surprise to be hearing it; he had been beaten with it for so long now, it was inevitable that some version of it would have rooted itself inside of him.

Do it.

A forlorn and already destroyed figure of a man, he couldn't take another step. His height and substantial girth hung awkward, burdensome, his great shoulders sagged, his face fumbled already with the collapse taking a hold of his mind.

He watched mute and useless as Buttons was swallowed up in the long grass of the broken ditch, trailing a rat maybe. Even old, the dog had a turn of pace still. The wind stirred the wheat in the field, and then came the further ripple of his small charging force and the keen peal of his barking.

'Buttons! Come here, boy!'

McCarthy's voice was very small and at first the dog, happy at play, paid no heed to the call.

Louder then. 'Buttons! Here, boy!'

The barking ceased. A minute passed when there was nothing but the beat of the wind and the view of the small village and the harbour below, the dark horseshoe of the land cradling the brackish sea. McCarthy stood in foolish wait, the tails and lapels of his heavy coat flapping hard with the breeze.

Then Buttons appeared, his head hunched low with guilt. He approached slowly, the long grass of the verge hiding his legs. His best eye fixed on McCarthy, and his nose twitched with the sense of danger.

'You've been a good dog to me, Buttons,' McCarthy whispered. 'I'm sorry I have to do this.'

Careful not to make his movements too sudden, he raised the hatchet, blunt backside of the blade at the ready, and let the dog approach. Then he brought it down, hard.

It was odd, how it felt, to see in his mind how he crouched to one knee there on the road, Buttons moving to him like all the times before, that head raised and almost smiling for some affectionate gesture. And then how the hatchet fell, coming down hard on the skull, between and above the eyes blinding and already blind.

A last pathetic whimpering sound and then the collapse. Not like when as a child McCarthy had watched his father swing the sledge hammer for the cattle, not in that staggering way like wilting flowers. Buttons just dropped, straight down, his life lost between the stance and the soupy puddle of the road.

To see him there, matted with mud and spools of hayseed, he looked no age at all. His eyes still stared, the blind eye flushed dark again from the sudden haemorrhage, and his mouth hung open, the whelk-like tongue greying in the dirt. He was truly dead, but death had made him in a strange way young again.

McCarthy pitched the hatchet violently away. It made no great distance, barely clearing the ditch; men would surely find it in the months to come when it was time to bring in the wheat, and by then it would be rusted beyond use.

When his father died, McCarthy had cried. He remembered going out behind the barn and just crying until his throat ached. But that had been forty years ago, and he hadn't given in much to tears since then. Now though, he could feel them catching his breath and hurting his throat once more. Buttons had loved him more than the world.

Dead, the dog was surprisingly heavy, much more so than during life. He sagged awkwardly and it took a full minute before McCarthy could find a secure enough position to carry him the long way back. The wind was approaching gale force, and it beat him low. Random casts of rain, cold and hard, scratched at his face.

It's for the best. You did the right thing. Buttons was old. Blind and lame, worn out. That was no way for him to live. It's the best thing for everyone, Mac.

Bríd's voice in his mind had been sated. She could be gentle when she got what she wanted. He hated that about her.

GHOSTS

The Viet Cong soldier stepped out of the churning jungle mists, a floating silhouette that ached for substance. I had pulled the last watch, and sat crouched in my foxhole as the darkness slowly became that murky, shielded green of jungle dawn. Stagnant water clung to everything, and my filthy boots shone a blunt reflective black through the congealing stripes of mud. The rain had folded up earlier in the night and now there was nothing to disturb the solitude except the searing heat and the mosquitoes. The trees stirred all around me, softly percussive, in palpitations that matched exactly the beating of my heart.

It was sweltering beneath the poncho but I was too tired to disturb my settled rut. The growing white light of the hour was thickened here beneath the trees to a strange luminous glow, and alone, thinking about nothing in particular, I was in a state that encouraged the calm of sleep, the spicy air of unreality further emphasised by the gossamer swaths of mist which veiled the trail and snaked between the pine trunks and branches.

The figure was just a greyness in the congruent twilight.

I sat hunched beneath my poncho, its neckline pulled up over my nose so that only my eyes were exposed, and I busied myself by watching the beads of rain fall in little smacks from my helmet brim down on to the poncho's khaki plastic. Beneath the cover, my hands held a ready M-16 rifle, but in the idle way of a child tired of the game.

It was a shock to see the enemy suddenly so close. He was just there, this obscure, spectral figure, moving slowly, but with an assuredly fluent gait. He seemed unconcerned about the need for cover, but maybe for him the smothering tendrils of jungle mist were cover enough. Or maybe this track was his domain.

The terror that tore through me was sickening. This shape made so vague by the mist; it crossed my mind that it could just be a ghost. I was nineteen years old, which made me a man without feeling very much like one, especially here, on some long forgotten jungle trail, just waiting for yet another night to fall away. I didn't believe in ghosts, not then, but at that moment I think that I believed in everything. And if my age made me fearful then it also made me stupidly brave, which is why they have young men fight wars, I think.

I was afraid, terrified, but I was a soldier too, and coupled with my swelling fear was the urge to jump up and empty my M-16 in a freeing roar. I wanted to scan the area for others but didn't dare to look away. Instead, I swallowed hard to quell all thought, and let him approach.

The enemy filled the dirt path, and clarity stole his ghostly pallor. I saw that he was just a boy, younger than me, as young as fifteen maybe, or twelve, dressed in simple cotton black. Charlie, the soldiers always called his kind. VC, Victor Charlie. But just Charlie for short. He wore dark leather sandals, of the thong-strapped type which offered nothing in the way of concealment or protection, and thick leather or rubber soles that slapped the sodden floor of the trail with every easy step. The softening green backdrop made the skin of his feet, hands and face seem very white. It made me think of ghosts again and I tightened my grip on the gun.

He moved with a swagger that the war had not yet fully stripped away and he allowed his big dark eyes to probe the jungle's ceiling in search of sky, his mouth pursed in the kissing shape of a soundless whistle. His fringe was cut straight and low, perfectly uniform, but the back of his hair stood up from the place where he had passed the night. A rifle hung in a lazy bias across his back; I could see the stock protrude from just behind the sharp corner of his right shoulder and the barrel, lower down, by his left elbow. It was left to my mind to fill in the falling diagonal of whatever lay between.

When he was about twenty feet away, he hit a shaft of thin light and it was possible to see or maybe just imagine runnels of sweat trace courses from his temples down across his smooth cheeks. A thin moustache painted shadow beneath his long blade of nose, the dark hair wispy and fine. He smiled at some private thought or memory, a gesture that offered just a glimpse of his upper front teeth, the small, even whiteness of them. Then the smile left its breathy realm and rose to the satisfying audibility of gentle laughter. Only laughter, a small grumble of it, but astounding to my ears in its alien rawness. He rolled his head a little, his eyes closed for just a moment, and when they opened again they fixed themselves on me.

Time was made fragile, a paralysed wait before the heart began to beat again. There was nothing for either of us to do but stare, it seemed, each of us frozen with fear, each with our features stretched wide in a funhouse mirror image of the other. The VC's lips parted as if with the need to say something, but all they offered was a tiny pop of dryness. He reached for his gun, his hands almost hypnotically slow, his wide black eyes still huge with the fixation of the moment. Something inside of me had the thought that I could just let him kill me, that it would finally all be over for me, but his movement served to give my body release, and I squeezed down on my own gun's trigger. Not a leaping flush but the single manual pulse of noise that burst like a thunder crack in a cave.

Dimly, I could hear or feel movement behind, but the fading bullet's howl still carried weight, and felt like the only thing that mattered.

The trance between us held, a mortal lock. The Viet Cong boy's mouth hung open with the intention of a previous thought and his reaching left hand seemed welded to the rifle's barrel. The shaft of my M-16 dipped and from above it I watched a wet bloom spread slowly across this thin child's chest, taking the black cotton top a silky step darker. The mouth which had so recently held laughter drew closed and shuddered with the convulsion of a swallow, his long throat juggling the hump of his Adam's apple.

A boy that someone somewhere, and for reasons that made little sense, deemed to be my enemy.

Behind me, men were scrambling to their feet, called by the rifle; I could see them without having to turn, could feel their movement. They didn't matter. Needing to do so, I levelled my gun's barrel again and fired once more. The second shot had a bark, ringing slightly hollow. I had Charlie's chest in sight but the adrenaline rush of fear or excitement caused me to draw up on the target and instead of adding a second spreading bloom to the one already delivered, it was the face that this time bore the savage brunt.

There was an instant in which I could almost see the impact, the caving in of all that made this poor bastard who he was, whoever he was. And then he dropped, not backwards or forwards but straight down onto the black dirt of the jungle floor, a lumbering sack of weight, as final as that.

The guys spread out to cover the flanks, their eyes, still bleary from dreaming about home or about here, searching the striped darkness of the jungle walls. Soon though, it became apparent that the enemy had only numbered one, that I had scored myself a stray, and they approached the body.

I stayed back, glad now of my poncho's protective embrace. My hands, alive with a trembling beneath my skin, still gripped the rifle. I remembered such a feeling from my baseball days, and from hunting, the cold aftermath of an adrenaline prematurely spent, but those innocent things seemed a hundred years more than the months ago that they had really been. I forced myself to breathe, and tasted the jungle heat.

One by one the men approached until they had formed a small open-ended circle around the dead Viet Cong. Everyone needed to see. Some just glanced and moved away. Others lingered as if in wait for something more to happen, trying to get the full measure of exactly how much they could endure. And some trembled with an adrenaline of their own, the fervour that had so savagely ruptured their sleep and now had nowhere to go.

'He ain't pretty no more,' Cooper mumbled to himself and cast a glance in my direction before walking away, his eyes tight on his black hands. Cooper, who would last only a fleeting fortnight more himself.

'Effin' car crash, man,' Kelly roared, and spat out a peel of laughter that sounded maniacal in the quietness of the hour.

But most said nothing. They recognised that death was near, and they respected that. A long trail lay ahead, this day and the next. Weeks and months more of trails just like this one. And this could be any of them, they knew. So they looked for a while, and then they moved off to eat some breakfast and to get ready for the trail again.

'You okay?'

I raised my head; it was the upward swim from the bottom of a dream. And Crow was standing there above me, his hulking frame bringing shadow even in this place of scant light. He was a shade of brown that was almost white but still wasn't, and in my mind I can see even now the man's big bare muscular arm with the fresh band-aid fixed to the swell of his shoulder. His Purple Heart wound, he liked to boast, smiling whenever anyone teased him about it, about the nick he had taken from an enemy bullet and then cultivated in all the months after, claiming that knowing how close he had come helped to keep him sharp. Maybe it was even true.

There was nothing to do but to shrug to his question and nod.

His big hands worked at a joint, needing no guidance, knowing the way. He raised his work to his mouth and licked the paper's edge, then let his fingers finish the job.

'You sure?'

I cleared my throat and tried to sound nonchalant. 'Yeah,' I said. 'Sure I am.' It didn't really work but it was the best I had, and I think he knew it.

Our stares fell away, to settle on something distant.

He stood there for a minute or more, Crow, called that I think so that no one would forget his colour, even when it wasn't always that obvious, and then he fixed the joint in the clenched corner of his mouth and snapped open a zippo. His tour was almost over; he had been In Country a long time and was waiting now for a rear echelon posting. I watched the leaf of flame lick at the paper's end and smoulder red. The guy drew deeply, held his breath and let it seep free in a series of stuttering hitches. White ropes of smoke crept from his flared nostrils and were lost in the gloom. He nodded to himself at last.

'Well,' he said. 'Take it easy, kid.'

'Yeah,' I muttered, partly in reply, partly in thanks, but Crow had already turned and walked off, intent on other business.

The dead boy gazed up at the slash marks of sky through the branches of touching trees. Someone had turned him over, probably with the toe of their boot. They wouldn't know why they did it except that some part of them needed to quench the terrible curiosity.

Kelly's words sounded off with such clarity that I almost shot a glance around to see where he was standing. It was in my head, but that didn't make it any less real.

'Effin' car crash, man.'

And he was right; there was some of that same need. It was a bad thing to see: a wreck on the highway or a boy without a face stretched out on a black jungle trail. A haunting thing, aching with the promise of nightmares, but it was a thing that had to be seen. You could look and then look away, but you had to look.

The bullet had opened up his face. His eyes were wide

and held captive the final fatal glimpse of horror and pain. The white of the left eye had flushed a shade of red that was slowly darkening to black.

I did that, I told myself.

The fringe still lay matted to that pale forehead but, leaning in to look close, I could now see tiny parallel worry creases, three of them, fine but emphasised by dirt. The close look was a punishment, and I felt like I was looking for some lesson, as if this should be too much of a thing to forget. The dead boy's face yawned in a soundless black pit, his nose and mouth reduced to just white shards of bone amongst the grey and yellow pulp of brain tissue and congealing blood. His lower lip was gone, and the exposed row of perfect teeth offered up to me the worst half of a terrible grin.

'All right, fellas,' the lieutenant, Rollins, barked at last. 'Get your shit together and let's move out.' So we did. We fell into formation and took the trail east, following coordinates that meant little to anyone and nothing at all to me. But we had to go somewhere, and every direction held its own box of magic tricks, its own particular brand of poison, so really, it didn't matter very much. East was just as good as west.

Everyone glanced at the kill as they passed, and I did too.

It was him or me, I told myself, or some voice did. He'd have done the same given half a chance. But there was something in the tone that didn't quite ring true. I had no grudge against this boy. I didn't want to be here killing men and children on the simple premise that they would do the same to me should the opportunity present itself. I'd learn in the months to come that they would, that they'd lie in ambush and give me and my comrades no chance at all. They had hatred in their hearts for Americans and to survive I knew that it was necessary for us to hate them back. And some did; the survivors, mostly.

I didn't hate them, even after I had seen enough atrocities by their hand to hate everything and everyone, and to never know a proper night's sleep again. I didn't hate them but I killed them. And the first was this Viet Cong kid on some damn jungle trail whose name I'd never remember and probably never even knew.

'You sure smoked that mother, Scruggs,' someone up ahead said, loud enough for me to hear, and someone else laughed at that. It was a joke, got so that it had to be, if we were going to keep any kind of hold on our sanity.

But I made no reply. I was thinking about ghosts, and how I had just sent another ghost to walk in this cursed jungle for all the time to come.

IN EXILE

Even on the mornings when the details prove elusive, I know when I have been dreaming of home. The first time I open my mouth to speak, I know. The words feel awkward and ill-fitting to my tongue, and it is clear to me that I have been dreaming again in Irish.

'Good morning, love,' I say, when Jenny, my wife, emerges from the bathroom all scrubbed and perfect and ready to face the day, and I have to stifle a gasp at the words. After such nights and dreams, this simple greeting always feels awkward and untrue, and the old words tumble towards the surface instead, the rugged dialect of the island which bears little or no resemblance at all to the bookish Irish that they teach the children in schools nowadays.

Nobody speaks Irish here in Dublin, it is a language as foreign as Swahili and as dead as Latin. But back on Cape Clear it was all we spoke. We had some English for dealing with the mainland, but it was broken and barely functional, like so many of our things, and it never felt quite right to us. I learned how to read and write and speak English in school, the first generation of my family to do so, the first to really be exposed to any kind of schooling at all, and at home I would do my homework aloud by the light of a kerosene lantern or else spread out on a piece of old rug before the fire. My sisters would watch me, fascinated, as they darned socks and mended the seats and knees of our trousers, understanding some of what I said but not all, and for their benefit I used the tone of casting spells when I read aloud, having quickly come to know the power of the words. It was a party trick though, and finally I'd grow tired of teasing them and we'd all sit around the fire and wait for Pádraig, my brother, to return from his day at sea.

What's past is past. I have some family there on Cape Clear still, but those obligations are easily met with a letter two or three times a year and a couple of hundred euros in a card at Christmas time. The island has closed its heart to me, and yet, despite the comforts of my life now, it can still feel very close. The bare stone walls of our cottage seem at times only a breath away, or the big window coated with the salt and grit of the sea wind and whistling drafts where the sealing putty has dried and turned to dust. I can feel the heavy wool of an old sweater, a thing belonging to my brother or my father, the thick shape of it sagging around me, and it fills my mouth with sweetness, that itchy taste so familiar. And when a storm is blowing and the wind catches the eaves just right it can almost pass for the high keening of one of my sisters singing something ancient as she busies herself with the chore of collecting breakfast eggs from the small coop or struggles with a slopping pail of water from the communal pump at the bottom of the hill.

We eat muesli now. Eggs are high in cholesterol, and muesli is good for the heart. Bacon is like a swear word, and I have almost stopped using it. Jenny wants me to switch to one of those pro-biotic spreads and I suppose that I'll give in, but not yet. Healthy diets are all the rage, but I am still holding out on some of the little details.

Jenny knows that I am prone to vagueness, and when my attention slips she understands that is where I have gone. Home. She doesn't have the same depth of feeling about her own home, Galway, but I think that is because any city, however quaint it may be, is just a degree of Dublin, or London, or probably even New York. She misses her family, but she speaks to her mother once or twice a week by telephone, her sister too. Her brother lives in Manchester, but even he is less isolated from her than my own people are from me.

Coming to terms with the pace of the city is not easy, but who ever said it would be? I'm just an old dog, I suppose, but I'm trying. Dún Laoghaire acts as my half-way house, my watered-down version of the reality; devoid of greenery, yes, but away from the worst of the bustle too, and I need it that way. Even after eight years, I can't help but feel surprised at the pace of this world. Torrents of people, the seething hum of engine noise, the chorus of horns blazing as a car dares to cut lanes; it is all so relentless. Taking my place amid all of this, I feel the way all refugees must feel, wandering along in a strange place, even those of us who choose our exile.

I saw him on a Saturday in February, on a bench in the Phoenix Park, hunched down into a thin Mackintosh coat that looked wet through. A mist was falling, a grey veil that brought frowns to many faces but didn't bother me at all. It gave the city a certain mystique, and its drabness reminded me of other misty days that I had known beside the sea. I was upon him before I realised, but he didn't see me and so I hurried by.

Later, I was content to stand waiting with our son while

Lucy took the few minutes that she needed to browse for Country music in Virgin Megastore. Luke looked too big to be in the light canvas stroller, and the way he slept with his head lolling to one side made him seem far removed from his childhood. I had seen old men sleep in just that same way, with their mouths slightly open and their hair mussed from the day. His eyelids fluttered softly beneath the drone of mindless speaker music, and his red lashes darkened from being pressed together. I told myself that it couldn't have been Pádraig on the park bench. He was back on the island, just as always, working the sea by day and then at night rattling around in the old place, the last of us inside those walls now. Wild and gullible, wrong for the confines and fancies of Dublin.

But it was him, I knew. My only brother, the man who had raised me as a son.

The following morning I went back to find him. A sleepless night was persuasive. The chances of him being there, I told myself, were slim, but he was in the same place. Waiting. Hunched there as before, that thin Macintosh coat still looking soaked, his hands thrust so deeply into its pockets that he might never have moved at all. It hurt to know that he'd been sitting here all night, destitute, afraid of every sound, afraid to fall asleep. He was strong and able to fight, but in terms of the city he was as naive as a child and bad things lurk in lonely places once darkness falls.

A wine bottle lay empty beside him, side down and steadied from rolling by the slats of the bench.

'Pádraig,' I said, and he looked up slowly, waking from his thoughts. My voice had the tight air of long ago, back when I had waited shyly at the top of the road for him to return from work. I'd stand there for hours sometimes, throwing stones from the road's verge into the fields, and when finally I'd see him approach I'd run to him and take his hand. But it would make me shy, as if the distance that really stood between us, a distance of fifteen years, was just too great, and I'd say his name, Pádraig, in that same tight, airy way as now.

The mist had lasted through the night but then had dried up with the dawn, and now the sky was overcast but holding. A bleak light made the world ache with shadows. He squeezed one eye closed against the glare, and I stood waiting for recognition to dawn.

He cleared his throat before he spoke, and that also stirred some things in me from the old days, long put-aside feelings of familiarity and pity. He had always done that, I remembered, ever since I was a child. It was a habit of island men, having spend so much of their lives in a boat, breathing the corrosive air.

'Who's that? Is it Peadar?'

'It is,' I said, though nobody has called me that in years. Dublin has made me a Peter.

He smelled of damp, and wine, and his cheek was cut, the blood dried to a crust, but his frame was hard beneath the layers of clothes and the clothes weren't ragged, just well worn. I wondered about the cut, whether it was due to a fight or a fall. Both seemed possible, and equally likely.

In the car, he dipped in and out of sleep. When he dozed he looked just like Luke, with his head lolled that same way to one side. He was red-haired too; our gene pool is strong, I suppose. I drove out to Dún Laoghaire wondering if there was a lesson here, if I was somehow being afforded a glimpse of the future. Luke was only four, and born into a different world, but time goes by so fast, and things can change. Different things call to different people.

The radio brought him back; Traditional Hour, the moan and thud of fiddles and bodhran seeping through the car. He sat up straight, his eyes set on the road ahead, one hand patting absent time against his knee. Rows of houses passed us by, each one an exorbitant but necessary debt, the price of a metropolitan lifestyle. Such ideas would be incomprehensible to Pádraig, I knew, as indeed they would have been to me, once upon a time. We drifted along, huddled together beneath unfolding reels and polkas, and I made what must have seemed like random turns left and right, past layer upon layer of apparently identical estates, until finally I found our road.

'Grand place,' he said, clearing his throat. I paused with my key in the front door, looked back and nodded, then, embarrassed, looked away again.

'Peter?' Jenny called out from the kitchen. 'Is that you?'

I ushered Pádraig in and closed the door behind him.

'Where did you go?' she said, and then she appeared in the hallway, caught sight of the down-and-out stranger beside me, and stepped back, startled and confused. I wanted to say something, but there didn't seem room somehow.

'If you like, I'll only stay a minute,' Pádraig said, lowly, to me. 'I can easily catch a bus back.'

'Jenny,' I said, trying not to make it too formal, 'this is my brother, Pádraig. Pádraig, my wife, Jenny.'

He cleared his throat again and muttered a greeting. It hardly seemed like words at all, and I knew it to be Irish, our old slang usage, all the vowels guttural, all the consonants soft as water.

I stood between them, feeling the brunt of all the discomfort. Then finally, Jenny smiled, straightened her dress around her hips, and said, 'Welcome, Pádraig. I've heard a lot about you.' This wasn't exactly true; at best she'd heard mention of him, more his name than the actual details of his character, but I was grateful that she said it, and I think Pádraig was too.

For an hour or so we sat in the living-room and watched as he drank mug after mug of hot sweet tea and ate bacon, eggs and sausages. He ate slowly, clearly not used to it, and he didn't come close to finishing.

It was difficult to talk. Jenny tried to help by pushing back the heavy silence, and I let her take charge. She was a buffer, I realised, and we needed her between us. Piece by piece, she gleaned the facts of my brother's recent life, and it was like extracting little nubs of glass from a dirty wound. The fish were gone, he said, but what he meant was that he could no longer harvest them. He'd had to sell the boat. I nodded, understanding, and let him think that we believed it was because times were hard and not that we guessed the truth, which was that drink had taken it, and every other small thing of worth in his life. 'The trawlers have taken over the ocean. There's no room for the small boat any more.' Over the past eighteen months he had grabbed short-term work on other fishing boats, or digging the roads as part of a contract crew around the west of Ireland, or toiling in the engine room of an oil tanker. 'I'm going back on that,' he assured us. 'In a week or so, I'm lined up to go to Argentina. Last year it was a Nova Scotia run. We do six months on, six months off. It pays good, enough to keep me floating anyway.'

The flesh of his hands was red and scarred from hauling rope and nets, burned from the wind and gritted raw. The nail of his left thumb was three quarters consumed by a black bubble that was slowly working its way out, and the top two joints of his right index finger were missing, long since amputated by a running line. 'I was staying with one of the lads who go on the tanker. He's English, but he has a small flat out in Crumlin. He was putting me up, because it's only a fortnight. We're heading over in a few days, on the ferry to Liverpool.' He didn't explain why he was in the Phoenix Park, and I didn't want to embarrass him, or catch him out in a lie.

'Well,' Jenny said. She looked at me, but decided to press ahead anyway. 'You can call him up, this friend of yours, and tell him you're staying with us. I'll get a bath running and find some of Peter's clothes for you. That way I can get your things washed.'

'I'll go,' Pádraig said once she had left the room, and he braced himself to rise.

But I raised a hand to him and he stopped. 'You won't go,' I said, feeling bigger than I deserved. 'You're my brother. If you're staying in Dublin then you should be here, in my house.' He stared at me, his mouth shifting, but no words came and after a moment I gave up waiting for them.

On the island, everybody lived and died with the tides. The sea took my father. I was a child not much older than Luke is now, but the magnitude of the tragedy was such that fragments have remained ingrained with me. I can remember standing with Sheila out on the last bluff of land, hunched against the battering wind and then the great icy stones of hail as the storm that beat the sea inched slowly in over the island. Sheila held my hand so that I wouldn't stray too close to the land's edge, and we stared out at the churning bilge, watching for the trace of the boat coming home. I could feel her beside me whispering prayers to Our

Lady to bring them safely back to us, but I didn't want to pray, and instead I watched how the waves crashed and foamed across the jagged coastal rocks, how they roared as they hit and seemed to draw an answering crack of thunder from the distance. Spikes of lightning slashed at the dusk and made it brilliant, and after they had faded I could still see them alive for full seconds, my mind's eye scarred with them. We waited, but there was no sign of the boat coming home, just the turgid blanket of the sea and the low pulsing sky made a thing alive by the storm, and at last the hail grew so thick and hard that we were forced to go inside. Then we sat by the fireside and listened to the wind crying in the chimney, already lamenting the lost, and Bríd cut and buttered soda bread for us to eat, because she couldn't just sit, couldn't even bring herself to talk about it. She was the eldest in our family, and the kind who had to be busy or she'd just break.

Eventually, late into the night, the wind died. Over the hours, we had become so accustomed to its sound that the gaping hole which yawned in its absence seemed profound. Anxiety swept through us then, stirred awake by the irresistible sense of anticipation. While the hail beat against the roof's thatch we knew that the wait would continue, but now that the worst of the storm had passed, any boats that survived could dare to come ashore, dare to risk the rocky coastline.

I went to the window and there was nothing to see but darkness, but I knelt there anyway and watched, knowing that I'd probably hear any approach before I saw them. Until that moment in my life, the dark had held no fear for me. Now though, its secrets and threats felt infinite.

There should have been two sets of footsteps on the road

instead of one. I ran to the door but couldn't bring myself to step outside. The steps came slowly, scratching wearily up the incline. The wind had dropped completely, and in the silent night their sound carried a long way. Sheila and Bríd sat at the empty fireside and their whispered prayers found full sound, a singsong cadence of words that held such sweetness I couldn't help but be carried along.

'Sé do bheatha a Mhuire, atá lán de ghrásta, tá an tiarna leat …'

For an hour, Pádraig couldn't speak, and by then a hiss of light had broken in the east, just the smallest ugliest line of white beneath the lumbering bank of night's blackness. He shivered from a cold which had penetrated down into his bones and there was little comfort even after the fire finally took hold and began to blaze, or from the warm blankets wrapped around his shoulders.

'The waves were running twenty feet,' he said, and he had to close his eyes to speak because details of the room kept trying to distract him from the facts. 'We were drawing in the nets for home when the hail came down, and I thought we'd all just die then because they were like chunks of rock just punching at the boat. Tomás took one to the temple and it split him open to the bone and stunned him so that he couldn't even speak his own name. We had to put him under the tarpaulin with the herring to stop him from wandering overboard, and we tried our best to ride it out. It was so dark that we could make nothing out at all except when the lightning hit. There was no horizon, no direction. Christ, the sea never felt so big to me.'

Nobody had actually seen it happen. Tomás, my father's brother, was out of action, cleaved open and concussed by the hail, and Pádraig was down below, trying to bail out the flooded hold. The hull was contracting against the pressure, he said, the water booming against the walls. I would come to know that sound myself when it was my turn to go to sea, and I weathered storms so I can at least begin to imagine the fear and the sounds of this one.

My father was gone. Presumably swept overboard, either he lost his footing on the violently pitching deck or else had been taken by a broadside wave. By the time Pádraig became aware of his absence there was nothing that could be done, no way to tell how much time had passed since he had fallen in, or how far the swell had carried him, or in what direction. Pádraig managed to revive Tomás, and together they flailed around the boat, linking arms at the elbow, not wanting to separate, too afraid to be left alone, even for a minute, with the raging sea and all the rising ghosts that storms can bring. But only the pale glow of breaking crowns tempered the darkness, the scudded peaks of the waves like rolling mountains, and finally they retreated below. Outside and all around, the wind roared and the sea built and surged and threatened to capsize them, and they stood chest-deep in oily bilge taking turns to work the pump. Tomás, still bearing the brunt of his concussion, waded through his nightmares, but his body seemed to carry on of its own accord and the tendons of his strong back and huge arms worked the lever in relentless fashion while Pádraig braced himself against the hose, too exhausted to even think, but crying over what had happened.

I can remember the fear of my brother and my sisters, but not my own. Our mother had passed some three years before, taken by the scarlet fever epidemic which had swept the island, and now a storm had come to make orphans of us, but I was too young to really understand that and my thoughts instead were with the firelight and the shadows leaping layers of drama across the walls, and with all the faery stories I had ever heard.

Three days after the storm, fishermen from the mainland found my father. From the shore we watched one man steer while the other four stood at the stern, tall and silent, guarding the covered body from further harm. When they made the harbour, Tomás took the tossed rope, lashed it to the small jetty and helped them ashore. He thanked them in Irish and then in English when they hauled my father's body out of the boat, and pressed flagons of *poiteen* on each of them, all we had to give. The men didn't want to take our offerings, but finally they did, to appease us. They loaded the illicit flagons into the hold, concealing them beneath a pile of nets, but returned unannounced the following day with cakes and barrels of stout and a whole boiled ham. For the wake, they said, and the islanders welcomed them in gratitude.

Pádraig stayed three nights with my wife and I. He bit at his lip until it began to bleed and the trembling across his shoulders grew worse with every passing hour, and it was clear that he was in pretty bad shape. When I pressed a glass of whiskey into his hand he looked at me with a mixture of gratitude and embarrassment, and his breath bristled around the edges with a buzz that threatened worse. But it relaxed him, and caused him to open up to us. A little, anyway. He shrugged quite a bit, a gesture which seemed to be apologetic until it became so over-used and began to look like something else, and he talked of how in the boiler-room of an oil tanker it was possible to feel the sea right beneath your feet, and it got so that a man never knew whether it was day or night. Nova Scotia had been a lot like home, he said, especially on that cusp coming out of summer when it was not too cold yet but not too hot either. He'd shown men in a bar some fiddle tunes from the island; they spoke a dialect of Gaelic that was oddly similar to his own and they'd been able to communicate without having to resort more than two or three times to English.

It astonished me to think that I could have forgotten about the fiddle, because there had not been an evening passed on the island that didn't see him take up his place by the fireside, his boots tapping to the lead of his fingers on the neck and the bow ripping across the strings, and the sound of it so sweet as it was joined by my sisters' voices in sung lament. I knew how to play too, had learned from watching Pádraig and my sisters, but I haven't touched a bow in years. Dublin just doesn't move to the same rhythms, and there are other things now for me to make than music. Easier things.

'What was Peter like?' he repeated, smiling in answer to one of Jenny's questions.

'Well, he was never Peter to us, only Peadar. And sometimes he'd get to singing something and he'd forget the world was even there. He was always getting lost in songs, could always catch a melody in an instant, and he had the voice of a bird.' He looked at me. 'We always knew he'd go, just as soon as he had the chance. Sheila used to grow hoarse from calling him, but he'd be away down on the shore or else over in the fields trying to ride Callum's horse. Callum had the farm over from us; we'd help him in the fields at harvest time and he'd pay us in meat. He kept pigs and cows, and he'd slaughter them himself and sell them off to the other islanders. He had this old skewbald mare that he used to ride bareback around the island, and I swear the ould nag could nearly talk. What was it that she was called again, Peadar?'

'Róisín Rua,' I answered, and he chuckled.

'So, you haven't forgotten everything then.'

'There's still a few things I remember,' I said. I know that I only imagined the bitterness in his teasing, that I was hearing nothing more than the voice of my own guilt at having abandoned them all for education and other things that even now probably seem like poor excuses in their minds. As poor as they sometimes seem in my own mind.

'Ah,' he sighed, sensing my discomfort. 'The island's a poor hand to a gambler. You did right to get off, boy. Else it would only have finished you, same as it did the rest of us.'

'I miss it sometimes,' I said, not really believing it until that very moment.

'Of course you miss it. Isn't it your home? But it asks too much of a man. Or a woman, for that matter. You did right, getting off.'

This small absolution was all that he could offer in exchange for my efforts at hospitality. And maybe he even understood, because, after all, he was running too. He had an increasing problem with drink, yes, but he didn't really need the six-month trips to sea to ensure his survival, because a man of his capabilities would always find work in one of the other island boats. He was running, just as I had; it was simply more difficult for him to break the binds.

As soon as it could, the bottle took hold, but in a relatively harmless way. He'd begin a train of thought and then leave it hanging there unfinished, and he'd watch us with those pale eyes, not understanding that we were waiting for more. Or he'd slip from English into Irish and back again until what he was saying became utterly nonsensical. Jenny had some Irish, but not the free-based dialect of our island tongue. Still, she didn't seem to mind; maybe the single glass of whiskey was enough to do for her what it took a whole bottle to do for Pádraig. She clapped her hands in time when my brother finally began to sing, the music flowing from him as he leaned back with his eyes held softly shut. I realised with some surprise that I had been waiting all night long for this, for him to be done with words alone because they could never really tell the whole truth of who he was.

His voice had aged from the strong baritone I remembered. Everything had conspired against that lovely timbre, and what remained now was the sound of a life lived in all wrong ways, the stories pouring forth on scraping, wizened breaths. All in Irish, but better for that, because the way that the echoes of the words melded with the melodies somehow carried a connection with all that I had ever known, with the rocks and dirt, with the sea and the great sky. Pádraig's voice ached with every joy and element of sorrow. Eventually, I was drawn in, helpless to resist, and I put my own voice with his. Mine sounded far less assured, but I found the way forward by instinct, all of this too deeply ingrained in me to ever be fully forgotten. When I glanced at Jenny, she was watching me hard, and I sensed a little hurt, I think, because this was something new to her, something at which she had never even guessed. I had lived my lie too well, I suppose, but I put that aside, closed my eyes and held fast to my brother's voice just as I had once grasped his hand and made a broken promise to myself that I would never let go. In my mind I heard our voices dance together and then soar, and the stories of the songs unfolded, long narratives twenty and thirty verses in length that I could not have remembered if I tried but still somehow knew. Tales of tragedy on the sea, and tales of lost love and exile. In the darkness I had made, I was home again, back on the island. I could feel the comfort of my family around me, and I could breathe the clean free air and just sing follow-the-leader games with old ballads that our ancestors had known and maybe written.

When it came time to part, he insisted that I let him off at the bus station. He'd meet up there with that friend of his, he said, and they'd get a bus out to the ferry terminal. In a few days he'd be on the high seas. We talked about small things that we pretended were important, but we didn't talk about the wine bottle, or the cut on his head, and I think we both excused ourselves the Saturday.

The clothes he wore were mine. Grey denims and a still-good shirt, my second overcoat, the knee-length navy wool. That, at least, would keep him warm if there had to be other nights spent in other parks. 'Well, Peadar,' he said, and grinned. 'I'll drop you a line from Buenos Aires. Look after that young fella of yours, and that lovely wife. And look after yourself, too.' Then he patted the roof and drifted off into the crowd that had swelled around the bus station. I watched him go, and wondered if I'd ever see him again. He slipped between lines of people, that big heavy frame wrapped shoulder to knee in navy wool, and in a minute he was gone. On the way back out to Dún Laoghaire I told myself that I had done right by him and said a prayer, and the words came to my lips in Irish because that was how I had learned to pray. If nothing else, it helped to pass the time.

Things will get back to the way they had been before. I'll

go about my daily business, an exile in search of acceptance, somebody trying hard to change. And time will have its way. Jenny and I will press on, our son will grow, becoming more like me every day and even more like who he should be. He will want the things that children of the city want.

I promised myself that I'd write home more often, but already I am late with my Easter letters. They are half written, tossed in a drawer, and they're becoming increasingly difficult to finish. Everything I say about Dublin seems boastful to me, and I don't like to bring up the island.

A couple of weeks ago, we were walking along O'Connell Street when Jenny thought she saw Pádraig in the distance. For a moment, I thought it was him too. The man had his build, and his red hair, and he wore what looked like my second best overcoat, the knee-length navy wool. But the Saturday crowd was large, and in an instant the figure was gone. I said that there had to be more than one red-haired man in Dublin with a coat like that. Besides, Pádraig was somewhere out across the Atlantic by now, deep in the bowels of a tanker on its way to Argentina. Jenny still looked unsure, but finally she nodded. These days, we both understand that certain shackles are best shaken off, and that selective perception is an essential character trait if a person is going to adapt to the ever-changing world.

WAITING

It seems that I am always standing here when the snow comes, taking shelter on the back porch of my grandmother's house. The flakes fall hypnotically, sluicing through the blackness, raking the air. The island has a way of holding its breath so that the only sound to be heard is the easy rush of the low tide lapping against the shore, somewhere out in the night.

The boundaries of our world here on the island of Cape Clear once seemed defined by rolling seas and oppressive sky, but now a migration has begun. The city lights of Cork or Dublin lure many away with the promise of a life that seems better because it is easier. The O'Briens from across the island, the Riordans and the Murphy twins have all abandoned home to forge other lives, but there was a time when we would play together in the snow until the flesh of our hands turned blue and pinched, and our fingers bled from the cold.

When I was a child – one of twelve in our family – I'd steal away from the others to stand out here on my grandmother's back porch, and my heart would beat fast with the anticipation of tomorrow, of the fun we'd have, building snowmen, sledding, playing games of war. Now I am twenty-eight, and that sense of excitement remains, even though I can no longer act on it.

Eventually, I'd be missed in the house, and someone would come looking for me. 'Come inside out of that,' they'd say, my mother usually, or one of my older sisters, Nuala or Eilís. 'You'll catch your death standing out there. Come inside to the fire. The snow isn't going anywhere.' I'd follow them in, not realising until I felt the fire's heat against my face and hands how cold the night really was, and with a smile I'd accept the mug of cocoa that my grandmother offered. She always made the best cocoa.

It is said that, in her day, she was a fine singer. She has sung for as long as I can remember, but the voice I have always known is a withered one, tempered by age. She'd sit there in the corner of her living-room on a small three-legged stool, her back resting against the bare stone of the wall, and she'd close her eyes, incline her head and drift into song. Aching narratives, old island laments for men lost to the sea, or for those fallen in battle. We'd listen, tapping our feet to invisible time, and my sister Gráinne – who had the best Irish of us all, and maybe the softest heart – would cry as the stories took hold. I had enough Irish to follow, and I knew the words by their flavours if not exactly their meanings, but it was the voice that would draw me in. My grandmother's singing voice was so much stronger than her usual spoken way, which rarely ventured above a murmur. To hear her talk, no one would ever have guessed at the power concealed in those breathy words. When she began to sing, that power was less revealed than insinuated. I was a child and she was already old, and her voice rustled around the words, caressing them as her hard creased hands sometimes caressed my cheek in a moment of affection. I could feel the power, and it was there as I grew.

Now when she sings, the power is finally gone, and the

voice that always sounded both hard and soft to me is a mired sound, muddy and occasionally indulging in shapeless hush. She is confined to bed and, when we sit her upright and support her with cushions and pillows, the effort that it calls from her wizened frame is almost too much to bear. Lying down, she sings rather than talks, singing the songs we all know. We join in where we can, but softly, because it takes nothing at all to drown her out. She also plays games with time, and it can be difficult to keep pace with her.

A few years ago, an archivist came to the island. One of those studious types connected with a university in Dublin, he was part of a group who had set themselves the task of travelling the country to gather and preserve a dying side of Ireland's heritage. I was at home when he called, on one of my occasional sojourns back from what has these days become my life, working month-on/month-off shifts on the North Sea oil rigs.

He stood tall and drooping in my grandmother's doorway, a young man of about my own age, but denim-clad and pierced, trying to explain himself in the kind of Irish that they only speak in schools. Some of the men in the village had told him that if he wanted the old songs he'd have to come and see my grandmother. I'd seen the likes of him before, one of those upper-class proletariat types who take a pair of scissors to the knees of their newly-bought designer trousers just so they will fit in with so-called 'real folks'. His long fair hair bounced in curls around his shoulders and he wore a pair of round wire-frame glasses pushed right up to his eyes. I studied him openly and in silence until his act began to come apart, then I nodded and brought him inside.

From a battered leather satchel, he produced the smallest piece of recording equipment I had ever seen, a little silver hand-held box that cut the music directly onto a miniature disk, and for an hour my grandmother sat at the kitchen table and sang for him. She held her hands knitted together in the grip of prayer, her entwined fingers bent and red from arthritis, and she alternately closed her eyes or fixed them on me, while the words flowed of their own accord. Between songs she'd mutter the titles, sometimes translating and explaining them so that the visitor might better understand. A small smile of joy stretched the young man's lips but he didn't speak at all until it was time for him to catch the ferry back to the mainland, and then he thanked her. After he had gone we found an envelope that he'd dropped under the table. My grandmother's name was scribbled across the back, and inside, five twenties. New notes, still shining from the bank. He had been too shy to hand it to her directly.

When I hear the way she sings now, lying in her bed so frail and emaciated, I sometimes think of that archivist, and how much he would enjoy this. Not for the voice itself – because that is a whisper of what it had been that day at the kitchen table, and stands as nothing at all against what people say it had been back in her youth – but for the mannerisms and shifting emphasis that old age has brought. It is as though the best lessons were in the act of loss itself, the ones most worth learning. The manner in which she bends the words, tormenting the time-worn rhythms of each song's structure, makes it into a kind of Island jazz. Certainly, there is that same scatting sensation. A deathbed art is something surely worth preserving, I think, but I am alone in my appreciation. Gráinne cries as she listens, but she is no longer crying for the stories. My grandmother's voice is a worn nub of past glories, but in the sacrificed lucidity of the diction there is such faithfulness in the sentiment. There are still things worth lamenting.

We spend a lot of time here, my sisters and I, and we're waiting for the inevitable. The shifts I work make it difficult for me, because it is all or nothing: An entire month spent sleeping beneath this roof, followed by an entire month away, when my only connection is the weekly letter that it has become Nuala's duty to provide. Every time I have to leave, I lean in and kiss my grandmother goodbye, and I am sure this will be the end. Occasionally she smiles a weary smile of recognition; more usually she calls me Dan, her brother, or Pádraig, her husband. Or other men long since dead to her. It hurts to hear that, but I answer her questions anyway, and then I take the ferry across to the mainland, the flight, and the other boat, until I am cut adrift, away in the North Sea, with a country's distance lying between me and the island.

The oil rig can be hard work, and the constant back-and-forth journeying between there and home feels, at times, like a never-ending ritual of exile and redemption. But I have been doing it for more than seven years, and a man can get used to almost anything over such a length of time. On the rig, sitting on my bunk while the wind lashes the spew of the waves against the walls and the plastic windows, I tear open the envelopes as they come, fully expecting the bad word that has yet to arrive. I read of the arbitrary news from home, the usual tedium of small happenings in small lives, and tell myself I am glad she hasn't passed yet, that I want to be there when it finally happens. But actually, I'm not sure that I do. It would be so much easier if the letter did break the inevitable to me, because as things stand, there is no comfort in waiting.

When I am at home, I sit in the corner of the bedroom for long hours, some unread book held open in my lap, and my grandmother lies there among her pillows and sheets, sleeping such a bottomless sleep that it cannot be much different from death. Sleeping, or else singing to the ceiling in that guttural voice. Her eyes are no longer with us, her mind, withdrawn, no longer offering the occasional glimpses and reminders of better times. I sit and watch, and I hate that I am waiting for her to die. But that is the fact. For almost a year, nothing has changed. The details are exactly the same, and I am not sure what I expect to see. 'A watched egg never hatches,' Nuala says, when she comes to relieve me so that I might wash and shave and get myself something to eat, and I know that she is right, we all know it, but none of us want the old woman to be alone when her moment finally comes. With every passing day, though, the shell grows more and more fragile, and it has to be soon that the final crack will appear. Maybe it will be a good thing if the news is broken to me by letter, the words easily fitting there among the mundane rest.

The snow is so light, and yet so complete. It fills the darkness, flecks that compromise the sky, and in the morning all that lightness will have amassed a considerable weight on the world. I like to stand out here on the back porch to watch, because it brings the good things of the past close again. In my life, I have spent more nights under this roof than in my own home. Easily lost amid the clutter of eleven siblings, finding room for anything was a struggle. Here though, there was always room, and a welcome. My grandmother lived alone, and she seemed old even then, though until a couple of years ago she was a very able woman. I was company for her, she said, and she told my mother as much. So I was allowed to stay.

Her husband, my grandfather, died before I was born. I have listened to her tales of him, her descriptions of how he was so broad across the shoulders, and though not very tall, possessed of almost legendary strength, and I would have taken her words as fancy except that the stories have been confirmed by other old men of the island, men tucked in the late night snug of Flaherty's public house, coming alive only when the talk turns to long ago. Pádraig Dunloe, a man to row and row. Pádraig Dunloe, my grandfather, whose name passed down to me.

'Do you take after him, boy?' the old men ask. 'Are you a chip off the old block?' I shrug my own broad shoulders and let them decide for themselves.

My grandfather went the way of many on the island – yet another lost to the sea. A hurricane, to hear my grandmother tell it, but certainly a storm. Pádraig and his brother Michael, two days off shore, with nothing but a prayer in their little nine-foot skiff. The stories were told of how, after they were thrown overboard, Pádraig had battled the great swell and actually made it to within a hundred yards of the shore before exhaustion finally broke him and he was pulled under. This, at least, is an idea heavily coloured with exaggeration. My grandfather did surely struggle, but no one could have known how close he came to victory since neither his body, nor the body of his brother, were ever recovered. Just a story, but such an end sounded utterly heroic to me, especially given the fact that my own father, Eoghan, had passed in far less spectacular circumstances, the victim of a sudden, brutal brain tumour, when I was three years old. Nobody told stories about him, and when they spoke of him at all it was with the resigned sadness of lost opportunities.

My name, the same as my grandfather's, might have been the draw to my grandmother, somehow bringing the past alive for her again. Or it may simply be that she enjoyed my company. I certainly enjoyed hers. She could be very shy, and entire days often passed between us with nothing shared but a smile. But the darkness seemed to shield her, and at night she would talk, would tell her stories of times and people past, her words swaying effortlessly between English and Irish. And when talking no longer seemed enough, she would sing her songs for me.

The nights of my childhood were always best. Until it was time for bed we'd sit together in the darkness, just the two of us, and I'd listen while she sang, joining in where and when I could. There were many nights when some of my sisters would come over, and more than a few nights when they all came, my mother included. A feeling of real kinship filled the house then, with everyone taking their turn to sing. Everything we sang was in the style of our grandmother, either consciously or unconsciously. You could hear her influence in the phrasing and in the tone. I remember Christmas time as always having a full house at night, thick to the rafters with song as the rain beat at the window or as the snow fell across the island. It felt good to be surrounded by family, but it felt better when the time came for them to leave, when they rose to undertake the mile-long trek back to my mother's cottage. The old house had a lovely way of growing suddenly quiet, and we'd sit there beside the fire, my grandmother and I, not speaking, simply breathing in the warm smoky air and savouring the contentment of the moment. Seeing how the snow falls brings those nights back to me as though they were close still, and not lost forever.

I've shed my tears for her. To see her this way, ravaged to this uncertain state, does make death seem like a mercy. It was a mercy when it took my mother, some five years ago now, letting us remember something of what she was like before the lung cancer could fully break her apart. But when death will come for my grandmother, I'll understand that it is for the best, but I'll still cry because now, whatever her condition might be, I still feel as though she is here for me. I can talk to her and it doesn't matter that she no longer answers, no longer hears, and I can listen to her gibberish words, the simple blur of sounds to past things. And more than anything, I can hear the jazz-twisted growl of her old songs made properly ancient. She'll die, and I'll be glad that her pain is finally at an end, but I'll cry anyway, and I'll miss her.

Everything changes. They are building on the far side of the island. On Tadhg O'Brien's place, there is now a small huddle of summer homes. Concrete boxes with black slate roofs, built for comfort but also for the view. O'Brien's grandchildren no longer want to farm the land; farming is hard work here and there is quick, easy profit to be had in selling out to the mainland's rich. Soon that idea will reach us on the western side, and our views are worth even greater cash value, affording as they do the magnificent bloodstained sunsets of late summer, that last hour of a long day when the placid sea blisters and is set alight. When our time comes, we'll sell too. The past is never permanent, constantly overlapped as it is by the present. The people from the mainland will come and make our coastline home for two or three months of the year, they'll sit in the old pubs, sipping fine imported whiskeys and glasses of stout, listening with all propriety and tapping their feet to what must seem like the nonsensical gabble of the old songs. Going native, they'll call it, their way of unwinding until it is time to return to the mainland and the stresses of their city work. A few of the old stock will linger, press on and endure the usual winter toils, but they will become the exception rather than the rule, and they'll come to rely on the summer economy for their survival.

Such changes are coming, and quickly, but whether they will happen in my own lifetime, I can't say for sure. Certainly though, my grandmother won't live to see them. She may linger a while, but eventually she'll go, and sooner rather than later. She'll pass away and we'll mourn her, and there will be nights when she'll come to mind as nothing more than a vague sadness, because time heals that wound even as it brings others. She'll go into the ground with those of her people who have gone before, another finished seed for the stony dirt of the sloping hillside. And maybe a day will come when they will be digging a hole in that ground for me, or maybe I'll have long since said my good-byes to this place.

All of that is ahead. For now my place is here, waiting for another end. Standing on this back porch, watching the snow, the night has a calm and timeless sense about it. The sounds that make it through from the kitchen are the sigh of the kettle and the barely whispered talk of Eilís and my youngest sister, Cait. They are making sandwiches for yet another long night, and they talk about things of little or no consequence. The big issue, the reason for everyone to be here, goes unsaid, because there is no longer any need to speak of it.

A KILLER STORY

The thing about me is, I walk down the street or into a bar, nobody sees me as anything more than just another face. I'm nothing to look at; early forties, medium height, build leaning more and more towards thickset with the passing of every year. I suppose I'm not bad looking, but I'm certainly no Cary Grant either, or whoever it is that the ladies like these days. Johnny Depp, I guess. My hair is still relatively full, but I think that all the years of washing has washed the darkness out. I dress casual/smart, which is how I like it. Nothing too sharp, a nice suit but worn for comfort. Women still look, a certain type of woman, anyway.

Mostly though, I'm pretty anonymous. Average, I guess, is what you'd say, and average isn't so bad, is it? Not many people would know by looking at me how I make my living. I probably look like a salesman or something, your typical Willy Loman type. Those guys really do exist. Sometimes, if I'm out of town and trying to pass an evening over a few drinks, I'll play along to that. It's a part that fits me pretty well. I tend towards a hotel bar when I'm on the road, because that's about the best place if you're on the lookout for a bit of easy company, no questions asked, or none that require anything like truth for answers. Working at the scotch, slow but steady, and keeping up the flow of small-talk with some woman about my own age. A woman in town for nothing important, but made lonely suddenly by the road. In hotel rooms, loneliness can be catching. My routine follows a strict formula. Smiles suggested and nervously returned, the offer of a drink. Small-talk to beat the band. Her life in jigsaw puzzle pieces: sometimes single but more often divorced, the scrapheap desperation and the pinched wrinkles hidden by the poor lamplight. Pretty, though, when she smiles, and her voice kept low so that I have to lean in a little closer in order to catch the smoky allure of the words. Pretty, but in the way of memories, and hotel bars are made to encourage such a sense. The gloom brings her prime a little closer than it really is, and my own prime too maybe. I play the Willy Loman role, my salesman routine not yet dead but definitely dying. It's been dying for years, and that works best for me. I never quite believe that she falls for it, but I understand that she is willing to go along with it for a while, because it's better than the alternative, and there are things about her that I choose to ignore too. It's part of the game. If it is a game. Who are we hurting? We're ships in the night, and all we do is talk, the best way to beat the loneliness, no matter what anyone says. There are the usual promises made, on both sides, when we finally say goodnight, but she doesn't believe them and neither do I. She knows that I am not Louis Mackley, or at least that I am not Louis Mackley the travelling salesman, but she never for a moment guesses who and what I really am. None of them do, not the women I meet for a while in a bar, not people I pass in the street.

There are lots of names for the kind of work I do, but basically it all comes down to the fact that I kill people for money. I'll do a few jobs a year, more than enough to keep me. I am, by nature, a frugal type of person. I prefer to rent than to buy, because I move around quite a lot. Movement stimulates me. I don't need much, don't really like to encourage expensive tastes. I save most of what I earn; putting it aside for my retirement, my rainy day. I'm good at what I do, as evidenced by the kind of money that I can make from a single job and also by the amount of work that I am forced, for practical purposes, to turn down. I'm good at it, at killing people, and though I probably shouldn't say this because it is the kind of thing that will make even psychiatrists who think that they have seen it all run screaming into the night, the fact of the matter is that I enjoy it. I love to kill people, the whole process of it, thinking up ways for them to die, planning the best way to achieve my objectives, and then setting my plan in motion. Everything is thought out with the utmost care and consideration. Each one has to be perfect.

Of course, I'm lucky that I set my reputation in stone at a young age, showing my mettle with a particularly audacious mob killing. It brought me fame in the kind of circles that really matter as far as my trade is concerned, adulation and notoriety in roughly equal measure. All grist to the mill. Now I have been doing this for close to thirty years, and in that time I have found myself in all kinds of situations. Pretty early on though, I reached a stage where I had become financially secure, and so I could afford to be selective in the work that I chose to undertake. There are always two things to look out for: a job that will further strengthen my reputation, and the kind of fee that just can't be turned down. There are certain moral dilemmas too, of course, but I deal with that in the same way somebody who works in a factory that pollutes the environment does; I tell myself that I am merely a tool, that I am simply carrying out the formalities of a decision which has already been made. I have a certain skill, a rare ability, and I am only using the gifts which have been given to me. Nobody knows me, and that helps too. I work under a pseudonym. The people who hire me are aware of this, and they humour me as an eccentric. Maybe they're right. I love what I do, I am good at it, and I don't expect it is something of which I will ever tire. Such a tremor of excitement as I set the stage and watch all the pieces of my plan fall together as one matter of fact, and then the thrill as I make the kill. It is a hunt, and I am the predator. The perfect predator too because, more often than not, my prey is utterly ignorant of my presence. They lie there, drawing that final breath, and their staring eyes flush with the last glimmer of shock and incomprehension. The level of passion I find in the act, that great surge of adrenaline, will be difficult to give up, and yet I know that I will, and soon. Mid-forties is not old, not yet, but it is getting there. Any of these days now one of my senses may begin to fail, or my attention to detail may slip a notch.

Until now I have resisted all urge towards comfort, feeling that a barren life will help to keep me sharp. But more and more there are dreams. A glimpse of some distant land across a television screen and the yearning to see that place for real. Or the idea of making the hotel rendezvous a thing more permanent than its current heartbeat existence. There is a rare but surprising sort of comfort in such longings. My nest egg is safe, and sizeable enough to offer a pleasant retirement. There are times now when I go to work and the details, the minor and mostly unimportant things which I have for so long taken for granted, seem suddenly more like obstacles. I overcome them, but with an effort that previously I never needed to spend. It can be wearing. Not that I don't love it still – the excitement is never lessened, killing people is a drug that never lets you down – but I recognise the symptoms of unrest as the first steps toward making a mistake, toward a job going bad. I love what I do, but I don't want to be the fighter who steps into the ring that one fatal time too many. A year, I reckon, maybe two. No more than two, certainly. I will take my time with what I do take on, and I will only take the work that absolutely cannot be refused. Generally, if a client comes to me, he can well afford my asking price. I will give it that long, two years, just like I said, and then I'll find a nice place and settle down. Maybe even marry.

I've seen part of that fantasy. A home, up in Maine, a fishing village that fills up nicely in the summer months but empties out even better come the Fall. Right on the coast, but with a stretch of woodland to the back of town. I've been there – for pleasure, not work – just got the urge once to wander and somehow ended up there.

It was coming into winter and they were waiting on the snow that the cold had to bring. I stayed at a small guest-house on the edge of town and they were glad to have me, glad of my money. The woman who ran the place was nice, not pushy but making clear her situation just the same. Widowed, ten years now, her husband had gone down with his boat while out pulling for herring. That is the way of it in those parts. She was about of an age with me, nice to look at and with a lovely smile, a mile from the movie star models that carry waiflike on the breeze around the trendy parts of New York. I don't go much for waiflike. I had planned to stay a couple of days, but then I got to waiting for the snow, just like everyone else, and ended up there for the best part of a fortnight. Maggie, her name was, though I got the sense that it was usually Mrs Wainwright. Anyway, a few days in, she coaxed her father into taking me out for a spot of hunting, and after a few hours in the cold some barriers came down and I found that old man to be a great companion. He hardly spoke a word to me the whole time we were out but still managed to teach me the correct way to flush quail and to take them as they lit from their nests. After our first hunt we stopped by a bar on the way back to the guest-house, intent on putting away a few shots of rye. I was paying; the old man nodded and said what a natural way I had with a rifle. Night had a habit of falling fast up there, but that evening we still had a window of light left to us, the sky a red stripe off to the west. We walked back slowly to the guest-house, feeling the good heat of the rye welling up inside of us, and I knew that this was the kind of town in which I could settle down. Nothing fancy on offer, and the air of reticence could be crushing to any kind of enthusiastic spirit, but reticence was what I needed.

We hunted every day after that, Maggie's old man and I, and he was never anything other than that, Maggie's old man. I was Mister, when he addressed me as anything at all. After the two weeks, leaving was like surgery, but I had to go because there were things to be done, loose ends and all that. I promised that I'd return, though, and that I'd stay in touch. Maggie was like everything else about the place – strong. The kind of woman used to disappointment, I guess. But she smiled, and surprised everyone by kissing me. I scribbled down an address, something which I had never done before for any woman, and she already had my real name so she was already far ahead of the pack. She knew some things about me, probably had guessed some others. I promised that I'd write, and I did, regularly. Still do. For now I won't call what we had anything more than friendship, but I do plan to visit again soon. There is a little house up there, right on the water and up at the far end of town. Nothing fancy, whitewashed cedarwood in need of freshening up, a step above a shotgun shack. Things need tending, especially the roof, but when I saw it I knew that it was just the kind of place I wanted for my retirement. Now when I write to Maggie I mention it, hint at my plans, and it is on the market still, with little or no interest apparently. Maggie writes every week, and she talks as if I belong there. Maybe I do.

My work tires me now. I'm fine usually once things are under way and I can fall back into the grooves that experience has cut, but it is the looking out for work, trying to decide between jobs, that wears me out. I take longer and longer to decide, and I know that is a weakness, but what makes it worse is that I know if I turn down this job I will have to wait around for another. I'm almost there, have almost reached the figure that will set me up for all the time to come. Just a few more jobs, one year, maybe two. Until then, I'll keep looking around. And I'll keep writing. You might think that there are only so many ways to kill people in a story, but I have been doing this for years now, and one thing I know is that there is always some fresh twist which can be added to any tale.

ALL THAT JAZZ

'I'm from Poland,' she says, then immediately regrets it.

'Oh, really? What part of Poland?'

'Krakow.'

This is a lie, but it is better to lie than to say Poznan, because people have heard of Krakow and having heard of it they think, or feel, that they somehow know it. Recognition always dawns across their faces. Saying Poznan would just offer an opening and invite conversation, and that always leads to complications. Jazz drips from the walls, stuttering piano that clears the way soon enough for a brushy, convoluted drum solo. It is live, but echoey here in the bar, leaking through the wall and the crowded doorway from one of the hotel's four performance rooms. This is a room for the serious Jazz, the eclectic stuff that she just adores. But the bar is crowded and nobody seems very bothered about what the musicians are doing up on stage. She tells them Krakow, any who ask, because it is a game, a way of keeping the predators at bay. 'Can I buy you a drink?' This one is an overweight, ruddy-faced man in his forties and maybe even his fifties, which makes him ten years or even double that too old for her. He has red hair clipped short. Tufts of it rise from the ugly puce flesh of his scalp, in a shade of copper that in this light seems somehow pale. He leans in as his kind always do, and penned into this bar room there is nowhere to go, no escape. She nods, not wanting a drink at all, but this too is the way it always is. Five or ten minutes later, there is a hand on her hip, drawing her close again and again, despite her polite efforts at struggle. Every move is a leading question. When he speaks it is right in her ear, shifting his body so that he can rub some of his weight against her shoulder, and he makes a gesture with his mouth that he seems to consider works as an apology; he can do nothing else but push this close in order to make himself heard above the noise of the room. All she wants is to be away. Every word she utters to a man in this place is taken for an invitation. He asks for her number, then thinks better of it and pushes his own at her, ornately embossed on a little saffron business card, and asks outright for a date. 'Call me,' he says, 'and we'll do something. Dinner, maybe.'

But that is not the end; his hand is still on her hip and maybe her gyrated efforts at escape have only encouraged him more, because he hasn't yet given up on tonight. When he leans in again she braces herself for more words, some other sordid invitation or proposition, but he chooses to forego the chat-up line and instead presses his face into the hollow of her neck. His hot damp breath coats her throat and cheek with a stale Guinness stench. She wants to cry out, but doesn't. She is here for the music, maybe the only one in this room who is. But she is lonely too, and after a second or third glass of beer she begins to feel a creep of exhilaration at the idea that someone wants to know her, even someone like this, a man old enough to be her father and one whose only attraction to her is his heartbeat. It is easy to push away the thought that he would be happy to know any woman tonight. The room is full of women, but a

Pole just seems a little more exotic to him, she knows, some small detail that can be bragged about to his work-mates on Monday, and with just a little more enthusiasm than usual. In comparison with the other women in the barroom she is dressed very modestly. A couple of girls push past, arm in arm and swapping gales of laughter. They can't be more than twenty and, in skimpy dresses worn too short and far too low-cut, their exposed flesh seems to glisten. They laugh the laugh of the drunk and uninhibited, tossing their long strawberry blonde and brunetted hair and baring their perfect teeth and then the enticing flicker of their tongues. They are on a night out, and the Jazz festival is the place to be tonight, the place that has drawn an influx to the city from all over Ireland and even beyond. It is a place to be seen, the perfect Sunday night platform for their talents. They laugh, a little bit drunk, and totter along on stiletto heels, knowing they have the attention of everyone they pass. And then they are gone.

This balding redhead's breath is slick against her neck and she tries to shrug him off. She is not those girls; for one thing, she is thirty, and beyond such needs. Even when she was twenty though, she was never them. She is simply dressed, in black faded denims and a light grey wool sweater. It is warm in here, but it is late October too. Her style is simple, but alluring in its way. She is slim and fit, and the clothes hug her shape and emphasise it with a worthy boast to all who care to look.

'I have to go,' she says, suddenly angry. With effort she pushes him back and if he is slow to understand then at least he yields. 'I have to meet a friend upstairs at ten.' She has lived here in this city for nearly six years. Her accent is still instantly noticeable but her English is excellent. Six years here, a mother of one, the best mistake that she has ever made and the price she has paid and still pays for the foolish illusion of love. She has been through this before, and nobody gets into her bed through the pity door any more.

DELIVER US FROM EVIL

It was late, after midnight, when the telephone rang. Joe Leary, already knowing who it was, sat up in bed, his chest tight with fear. He lifted the receiver in the hollow between the third and fourth metallic chime, raised it slowly to his ear and listened.

'Yeah?' He clenched his eyes shut, hoping that there was sufficient brevity in one syllable to hide the quiver in his throat. When he opened them again, the bed-sit seemed a little brighter.

'You got the note ...'

Though he hadn't heard it in more than five years, the voice was instantly recognisable to him, cutting through everything, right to the bone.

The talk that followed worked mostly in silences, punctuated only with the rooted code of words carefully designed to guard against tapped lines and unwanted listeners. The caller's tone carried the same high lilting familiarity of years before, with the rounded vowels and the drawn consonants, a voice so foreign here in England but kindred with his own.

'I did.' One upper wedge of the window's glass held some of a streetlight's orange spillage, and rising from his bed to stand, Joe could see needles of rain streaking through the unearthly glow on a slight diagonal.

'There's a place, The Hawthorn Bar on Xavier Street.'

'I know it.'

'Lunchtime, then.'

There was a moment of trying desperately to think of something to say, some way to scream, *No, for Christ's sake, haven't I given ye enough?* But no such way offered itself, only a stranger's acceptance coming from his own mouth, and all that remained then was to wait for the lilt to rise again.

When it came though, it held only the false nostalgia of, 'It's been awhile, Joe,' and after a few moments of breathy stillness, he found himself listening to the tinny in-and-out drone of a broken connection.

Growing up on the Falls Road, it was hard not to take a stand. Most of the men on his housing estate were died-in-the-wool types and staunch in their treason, their destinies marked and their hatreds defined virtually from the womb. Joe's way in had been different, and probably all the more dangerous for it.

His father, Tommy, was a man who had never raised so much as his voice in anger, at anyone or anything. A bus conductor who existed in a war zone and yet seemed blind to all manner of bigotry, he lived the simple, ordinary life of a husband and father. He enjoyed a pint of stout in the social club on a Sunday evening and maybe a game of rings or a few hands of Forty-five, but he was always just as content to play his old squeezebox melodeon by the fireside on a winter's night while the kids sang the songs of generations past. Joe recalled often how the old man could make that accordion cry; he had a version of *Carrickfergus* that could pull a heart asunder.

It was a British soldier's plastic bullet that had torn open his throat, and that was the way of things in Belfast during the bad years of the 1970s. The street cordoned off, seven soldiers watched him take twenty minutes to die, him slumped and gasping in the muddy gutter between road and footpath, and four hours later they approached to prod the body with the polished toes of their black boots and to mutter sympathy for the poor bastard, whoever he was, their machine guns levelled and at the ready, just in case.

Dead, his staring eyes held fast to the charcoal shell of his hometown sky and the blood slowly crusted around the wound in his throat and stained the wet tarmac with a shining darkness. An accident, they said, a tragedy, as Tommy Leary joined the growing list of fallen innocents, he perhaps the most innocent of all.

From then on there were father figures all along the Falls for the eleven-year-old Joe. His every breath, sleeping and waking, took on a bitterness, and hatred found an easy foothold, intensifying over months and years like a slowly acting poison in the bloodstream.

There was an allure about the movement, a camaraderie, a strong feeling of place. 'Your father was a good man,' they all said, everyone, men and women alike. 'A bed in heaven to him.'

But it was Dan Keogh who drew him in. Dan had been in his thirties back then, a tall thin man with slightly hunched shoulders and a growth of golden beard cropped closely in to his gaunt face. He had sharp blue eyes that smiled only for Joe and for his own child, Bríd.

What followed had the echoes of a second schooling, and at the age of sixteen Joe's graduation to the rank of active soldier was marked by an ambush on a border patrol. Dan had accompanied him, and another, a man of about the same age, named Mick Scott, brought in from Tyrone for the job. Joe remembered how he had been terrified on the way, but how impressed he had been too, at the way the two men laughed and chatted easily about other men they knew. As if the end of the road held nothing more substantial than a game of bowling, or a hurling match. He sat alone in the back seat of the Ford Cortina, sucking in deep breaths as they passed through a string of small villages, and trying in vain to catch some of the men's carefree manner.

And then, in the darkness, lying in the long grass at the edge of a wood, it seemed like a dream. He heard words, or felt them in that odd dreamlike way, Dan whispering instructions to get ready, to aim low, and not to stop until they were all down or until he was told that he had done enough. Other things too, unimportant things, lost in the stuttering flail of automatic rifle fire, and sparks that lit up the night for frozen heartbeats.

Later on, in the back room of some friendly pub in the small hours of the morning, the older men recounted again and again the details of the ambush, and there was much back slapping for Joe, who put down whiskey after whiskey in the hope that it might burn away some of the numbness. All three soldiers, Dan said confidently, and there was singing until dawn. *The Rising Of The Moon* and *A Nation Once Again*; all the usual songs.

'Don't read the papers or watch the news for a few days, lad,' Mick had told him in a quiet moment, leaning in like it was good advice. 'What they say is all just propaganda.'

Over the next few years, it was more of the same, until

the people of the Falls began to look at him as they looked at Dan. He saw first hand the horror stories of the British soldiers' actions, the women and children shot down like animals in the street. It was war, just like Dan said. And when they asked him to leave a package in a Loyalist pub, he pushed away any doubts and did as he was bid. It was just a warning, Dan had told him, no one would be hurt. And he was right; when the place had gone up in the small hours, nobody was even in the area. But the message was clear, just the same.

The hours until lunchtime were long. Joe lay on his bed through the night, fully dressed, watching the window and the scattered rain and thinking about his past. He wondered if shame was enough to kill a man and whether or not there could be salvation for someone like him, either in this life or in the next. He had not prayed in many years, or at least not in any meaningful way, not since he was a boy. Now the thought of prayer held a kind of comfort, but even as he tried to find a way back in, the hypocrisy of the act made it feel almost sinful. He was ashamed, but he had done what he had done and he would do it again, not because it was what he wanted but because it was what he had become.

When morning brought a glossy sheen of daylight, he got up, washed in a basin of tepid soapy water and shaved by the small square rust-speckled mirror that hung on one wall. The kettle slowly boiled for tea as he scraped away the night's stubble from his face with a throwaway razor. The reflection in the mottled glass was of a broad-faced man with a sallow complexion. The bones of his face were heavy beneath his stretched skin, the strong jaw and prominent cheekbones giving him a fierce look. He raked the fingers of one hand back through his hair. Tawny in colour, it was growing out of a crew-cut now and receding fast.

He had changed a lot from the boy that he had been back in Belfast. Even more than the two prison sentences he had endured, the running life had made him hard, the things he had done and the places he had been, always alone, existing like some low beast.

The radio played old songs, none of the stuff he liked, but he listened anyway as he made the tea, to the music and the idle chatter of the disc jockey. He crossed to the window a few times, but the street was quiet, a typical Sunday morning. On the table by his bed, a small cherry red alarm clock pulsed away the seconds and he watched the fast hand chase its way around and around toward half past nine.

He polished his boots and distractedly read for a while a ragged copy of an old Louis L'Amour novel that had been left behind by a previous tenant. The covers had been torn off so he didn't know the name of the book, but he supposed it didn't matter all that much. And he only knew that it was L'Amour because of a short biographical spiel on the first page. He read without absorbing much of the tale, and then, as the time approached eleven, he ate sardines in brine and cold baked beans straight from their tins. Not exactly gourmet, but he had endured worse. He could have heated the beans, could have made tea even, but there was a kind of necessity in feeding this way, everything cold and slick and straight from cans. It all served to hone that edge once more, to sharpen his instincts for whatever lay ahead.

Coming on for noon he gathered up everything, any clue that might hint at who he was, anything that might hold a print that could be traced at some later time, piling it all into a plastic bag. His own belongings were scant, just a couple of shirts, a spare pair of jeans, some underwear and his shaving things, and he packed them all into his small rucksack, one that had accompanied him on many years of travel. He scanned the empty room, hating suddenly the depressive atmosphere of the place, the hollow gloom like slum disease, and he was glad that he'd be leaving behind the debt of a fortnight's rent.

Bríd had loved him once. He was sure of that. They had grown up together from their early teens, and at times she had seemed almost like a sister. Almost, but not quite, because there was a thing between them. An electricity, he supposed it was, the blossoming of some thing like love. At fifteen she had kissed him on a dare, and after that he was hooked. She was everything he wanted, his ideal.

About 5'6', a good height for his own, coming on for six foot as he was, she had jet black hair that she wore to the shoulder sometimes but more often pulled up into a loose ponytail. Tied up like that, it better suited her pale complexion and the delicate structure of her face, gave her a sleek, angular appearance. He loved how her cheekbones had such strength, and her eyes were large and a shade of jade that seemed to play sinful illusions with waning light. She smiled best of all for him, and she had a way of understanding who he was, what he was about. She had her mother's looks, Dan said so and it was true – Maura did boast those same eyes and wonderful bone structure – but there was little doubt in anyone's mind that she was her father's daughter.

After the ambush she had come to him, and though he knew better than to talk about it, even to her, she seemed to sense it in him, and it tightened whatever it was that they had together. She was a woman of the movement, even as a child, and the way she talked seemed to make his acts heroic to both of them. Dan had never encouraged their friendship, but he had never actively opposed it either. When they became lovers, people must have known, or at least suspected; on an overcrowded housing estate, secrets were difficult things to keep. And if people knew, then Dan must have had some inclination too.

She was two months pregnant – the greatest secret of all and one that they *had* managed to keep – when a bomb tore apart the local shopping precinct, an act of Loyalist repercussion in answer to who knew what slight, just one more round of an endless circle. Seven people had died on the scene, and Bríd became the eighth victim after fourteen hours of desperate emergency surgery at Belfast General. Joe sat in a cold white waiting-room with Dan and Maura, his world coming slowly and irrevocably apart.

When the surgeon finally emerged and said how sorry he was, that they had done everything they could but that there was just too much brain trauma, Dan pinched his mouth tight, nodded and squeezed his wife's hand. Only Joe cried. He was young still, and dealt badly with pain.

The funeral drew hundreds of mourners. British soldiers skirted the graveyard in an effort to ensure a tenuous peace – they knew who Dan was, where exactly he ranked in the movement, and they built connections with other faces in the crowd – but despite their presence, two young Loyalists managed to secure good vantage and threw stones from a tree, blew an air horn and chanted disrespectful slogans. The soldiers could only watch as the youths were chased and caught, one beaten into a coma, the other into paralysis. Joe stood beside Dan, trembling with rage and fear, watched as they laid out the Tricolour over the coffin and as the rifles were fired by the men in camouflage uniforms and balaclava masks. He ached inside, felt it as a clenched fist in his chest, the last ounce of his goodness suffocating.

Later, in the corner snug of their local bar, he told Dan of his situation with Bríd, how close they had been. 'I loved her,' he said, and Dan had only nodded, because he already knew. Carefully then, Joe broached the subject of the unborn child, and this at least brought some reaction, a hard minute of stare, Dan's shock pushing up through his own grief, reaching for understanding. Then he gritted his teeth and his face became a snarl. 'Use that, boy,' he said. 'Use it to make those bastards pay.'

He dropped the rubbish from the bed-sit in a series of litter bins along the streets. Careful as always. It hurt to think back, but sometimes he needed that hurt.

Memories of the day that Bríd had died – *was murdered*, his mind would have screamed once, but not now, not any longer – Bríd and his unborn child; such memories were the only thing of any worth that lived inside of him anymore. It was as though that day had been only yesterday; there was that same vivid sense about it.

He had been at work – he laboured with a local builder, the usual kind of thing, and he had heard the blast even from the building site more than a mile away, and everybody knew instantly what had happened and also that it would be bad, late morning as it was, and a Thursday. The only question was whose bomb it had been, which Loyalist faction would lay claim to the job. Not that it mattered, of course; differences and similarities were only for the politicians. They knew that it wouldn't have been a Republican bomb, because they would have heard about it beforehand but also because it was in their locality, right there in the Falls. A shopping centre. Christ. It didn't matter which finger of the same hand had pushed the button, because what they had to do to end this was break the hand itself.

Not long after, Dan arrived at the site. Looking pale and frightened, a way that nobody could ever remember having seen him. Joe thought that he was coming to talk over some plan of reprisal. Some of the other men must have assumed the same because work was stopped as they gathered around to hear what he had to say. The men who had chosen not to involve themselves in such things remained on their scaffoldings, but they didn't work, just watched from a distance, afraid.

Dan seemed to see nobody but Joe.

'Joe,' he said, 'I need you.'

The other men understood and began to step back, but they didn't move far because there was nothing kept quiet inside the walls of the movement.

'What is it? The explosion?'

A sharp nod. 'Bríd was there. They got her out, but she's at the hospital. We have to go.'

Dan's hand was on his arm, gripping, forcing him into movement. Like a dream again. So much of his life had been lived in dreams. Vaguely, he remembered that he was holding a spade – he had been mixing concrete – and he carried it right to the gate of the site before one of the other men ran after them and took it from him. He gave it up from his stupor.

Beyond that, only fragments lingered, barely connected

snippets such as the taste of hospital tea from a Styrofoam cup, sour and nauseous even with the splashed addition of Dan's whiskey sweetener, and the rustle of magazine pages to vie with the pulsing of a small analogue clock just above the door. People passed along the corridors and sometimes there was even laughter, as though this place was not a hospital at all, not a place of sickness and coming death. The shuffle of feet, snatches of conversation, but in the waiting-room there was nothing more than the numbing white light and the low sound of worried breath.

Dan had said lunchtime on the phone, and for a Sunday, noon would do just fine. He'd have had the place well watched, would know of its friendly bent to men of their kind.

It had been a long time since they had met face to face. Dan's was a face that Joe never wanted to have to see again, this man who once had been like a father to him, or a father-in-law. Joe hated him now, hated him for all that he had always represented and represented even still. A user, playing people like pawns in a game. And not just Joe but his own family too, offering them up as sacrificial lambs to the slaughter.

Time was, Joe blamed the world for Bríd's death, or blamed himself. With the passing of years he tried to persuade himself that it had all been mere circumstance, born into the wrong place and at the wrong time. Such beauty, it could still make his breath catch in his throat to remember her and how she would smile for him, but beneath that beauty was the fatal and deadly flaw of genetic bias. She had always been her father's daughter. Which was how, finally, Joe had come to lay the burden of death squarely on the shoulders of Dan Keogh. He had made her, cultivated the hatred in her heart, gave all that precious outer substance such a poisonous sting.

After all the rain, the surface of the streets shone with a kind of gloom. This part of the city was rundown, litter clogged the gutters and windows were boarded up on many of the buildings. There was a strong air of menace, but it was a good enough place for the damned to walk. Joe tried not to think of the past or of what lay ahead, but there was nothing else, it seemed. This middle ground, this present, was a limbo. A living death.

The call could only mean one thing, of course. They had a job for him. It had been a while since the last time, two years nearly, and the police had brought him in for that one but hadn't been able to make it stick. So he had walked, and kept on walking. He could remember that a part of him had wanted to go down; he had planted a bomb that had killed two people. Both security guards, but they had just been doing a job. Trying to make a living. He tried to imagine what it must have been like for them, that instant when the device was triggered. Had they even known about it, or in that instant did they understand everything there was to know?

A part of him had longed to confess; it would be his third time going down, and this time they would see to it that he was put away for good. But he was in too deep, even if it felt septic in his blood by then, the movement rotting him away from within, making him a time bomb, his innards all SEMTEX and nitro-glycerine. And because he was in so deep he had kept silent, even when the going got heavy, when they tried beating a confession out of him, three detectives with their hands wrapped in towels, focusing their brutality on his kidneys and his groin, or pulling his hair until his eyes watered and his scalp bled. They did their worst, but he was used to such by then. When they released him finally, he had run, staying nowhere very much longer than a month or two.

That was it for him. He had said so from time to time, but after the last job he meant it, told people in a position to matter. They had nodded, said all right, if that was how he felt, he had certainly earned his retirement. Maybe they could find work for him in a less active field, planning maybe, or casing. Of course, he was highly skilled at what he did, and they'd miss him, so perhaps he'd consider a sort of semi-retirement, where they were still able to call on him for work that nobody else could be trusted to undertake. Not risky stuff, but jobs that required his finesse. Nobody got out clean, he understood.

The bar was quiet for a Sunday, a dimly lit place that smelled of stale beer and the underlying tang of urine. There was sawdust on the linoleum-covered floor, soakage for spilled drink and friction against the slippery surface.

Joe stood a moment in the doorway, trying to let his eyes adjust to the gloom. He couldn't see Dan but he was certain that Dan would be watching him. He approached the bar, called for a pint of Guinness and let his fingers drum idle patter on the oak counter while the elderly bartender began to draw stout from the tap, angling the glass just so. Then he dug in his pocket, pulled the last note from the loose coins. A five pound note, all the money he had left in the world except for an emergency two hundred at the Ulster Savings Bank. He held it out but the barman just shook his head.

'Your money's no good here.'

Joe stared at the note in his hand, then nodded and put it back in his pocket.

'You can pour me a whiskey then, if that's the case. Just a drop of water.'

The man behind the counter had an English accent, but the set of his mouth indicated a different heritage. Joe watched him drag two tots into a water glass from the inverted bottle of Jameson above the cash register.

'Here, add the water yourself,' he said, filling a second glass from the sink. 'Men can be peculiar about their whiskey.'

Joe took the water glass and splashed just a drop into the whiskey. Then he swirled the spirit around to encourage the slight dilution. 'Just to take the purity out of it,' he explained, as the other man watched. Then he tasted it, sipping, and sighed his satisfaction.

Over by the large fogged glass window, three men sat over pints, their rough general appearance indicating that they made their living as builder's labourers. They had the soft brogue of Irishmen, and when one of them, a heavy-set man with a thick red beard, abruptly broke into song he had a gentle baritone, leading the way on a wistful rendition of *Galway Bay* for the others to follow. Even the barman leaned on the counter and joined in. And it was only as they drew the ballad to its natural end that Joe noticed the figure hunched into the thickest shadows of the bar's corner. He drained the whiskey in a long swallow and followed it down with a mouthful of stout, the fire of one lacing threads into the cold cream of the other, steadied himself with a breath, and moved across the floor to that corner table.

'Joe.' A smile but a surface thing, hardly worth the trouble. 'It's been a while.'

Joe stood, waited until the invitation was made to sit, and nodded. 'Aye, it has at that.'

'How've you been?'

He shrugged, because there was little point in answering. They were both far beyond such things, knowing each other as they did.

'You've a job for me, is that it?'

'We do. The lads felt that you'd be the only one able for it. The tube. We want to take out a line, hit the infrastructure, you know?'

'What is it, a warning?'

Dan smiled. 'If you like.' He had the smile of an animal on the prowl, something canine and likely rabid. 'We'll open up the place, use enough of the stuff to close it down for good and all. Piccadilly line.'

'When?'

'Soon as you like. But hit it for rush hour.'

'Rush hour. Jesus Christ, man. We'll kill thousands.'

Dan's smile never wavered. But his eyes were fixed and black. *Cross me and I'll tear the flesh from your bones*, those eyes said.

'War can be a bad business sometimes. And there is no one that knows it better than you and I. Am I right?'

'Jesus,' Joe said again. 'This is a lot to take on.' What he needed was time, to think about this, to find some way out of it all. He had done a lifetime of bad things but how could he live with himself after doing something like what Dan was asking of him?

'I understand how you feel, Joe. Really I do. I felt the same way myself whenever I was called on to do a big job. It makes it worse knowing that we're not hitting soldiers. And I know what it's like to lose someone I loved in just such a situation. You know it too. Maybe you know it more than anyone.'

This was nearly too much, having to listen to how he used Bríd in this way, even now after all these years, to coerce Joe into doing what he wanted.

But Joe knew he could give away nothing if he expected to find a door out of here. So he nodded, tried to fix his face with the distraction of shock. It wasn't difficult.

'Think of the conflict, Joe, the hundreds of years of repression. And think of men like you, men we sing about now. Sean South and Bobby Sands and men of their kind, men who sacrificed all they had for the cause. Or if it helps, think of yourself as one of those American pilots, dropping those A-bombs out in Japan. Theirs was a war and so is ours, Joe. Sometimes we have to do hard things in order to win. The end justifies the means. Try to remember that, hang on to it.'

Joe drank from his glass. Suddenly the Guinness in his mouth was like bile, as sour as that, but he drank anyway because it bought him time. If he said no, he'd never get out of here alive. It stunned him that there could be a comfort in such a thought, but rather than rest in it he pushed it away. Death was too good for him. Finally he lowered his pint, and looked at Dan once more.

'If I do this, can that be it for me? I'm not looking for out, but I can't go on with this kind of work. I can't sleep nights for some of the things I've done. Will you square it that I won't be asked to do any more? Bump me upstairs, executive position, something like that. I'll lick envelopes, for Christ's sake. I think I've earned a rest, don't you? And I want to come home.'

He didn't want to go home, wanted rather to get to the very ends of the earth. But he said it this way because it was all part of the game.

Dan clapped him on the shoulder. 'Don't worry, Joe. Do this one last job and I'll see to it that you won't ever be troubled again. And we'll get you home too, I promise you. I'll find you something with the party, something easy.' He paused, stared into Joe again. 'So, you'll do it then?' Joe could feel the grip of those eyes, and how they dug at him, into him.

'I will.'

'Good man. I knew you wouldn't let us down, you were always the best we had.' Dan turned, called out to the bartender for the same again over here. Joe caught a gesture, a nod of the head to the three labourers by the fogged window. They could relax now, they'd not have to earn their pennies this day.

The two of them drank a while then, and in the silence all the years of things that had passed between them seemed insurmountable. Joe couldn't help but think of Bríd, and of his unborn son. Maybe, he thought, Dan was thinking of them too; after all, his blood ran in their veins, his genes shaping them to his form. But somehow, Joe didn't think so. Dan would use them only to freshen his resolve, and like everyone else who had strayed into his life, they were to be used for a purpose and then cast aside.

'You have a place to stay?'

'I just moved out.'

A nod. 'All right, good. I'll sort it.'

'I'll need money, enough to get me away clean and in a hurry. It'll be six months anyway, or a year.'

'Money's no problem. And I can set you up with a few addresses. Where'll you go? The States?'

'I suppose.'

None of this can ever end, he thought as he made a run on the tube. Two days had passed, and Dan, as always, had been as good as his word when he was getting what he wanted. Joe found an almost empty carriage on the tube and sunk down on to the seat. Really there was nothing to see, this was only routine, to absorb some of the feeling of the job ahead. It would of course, be different at rush hour. All the carriages would be crowded to standing then. And it would bring a devastation the likes of which had never been seen before.

He knew the tunnels well enough, had worked down here for a while back in the early 1980s with an Irish firm contracted to install fire alarms. He had form by then, had been inside, four years, but so had some of the other men, and since they worked hard and cheap, nobody cared very much. Night shift, that had been, not that it made a difference this far down underground. Down here, night and day were the same halogen glow, the same bleakly lit platform tiles, the same endless stairwells. He had spent eight months dragging cable through the tunnels, clipping it to the walls, following orders, and he'd work and listen to the rats chase circles in the blackness, the acoustics making them sound as big as bulls.

That had been a bad time to be in London, the movement had dictated an escalation to the war and bombings were rampant across the city. He had needed his alibi of work more than once during that period. And it was a difficult thing to bear, listening to how those explosions rang around the underground, rolling through the hollows like the worst anger. The secrets of the city. And when they finally passed, the fill of night that followed was a deathly silence. Must be something like that in hell, he often thought.

People boarded and departed at the different stops, their faces blank, their minds already with the day ahead and with their own problems. Joe tried hard not to look at them, but they kept fixing their details to his mind. Tomorrow he'd be killing them, or people like them. The lucky wouldn't know what had happened, those on the right carriage, or the wrong one. The scene would be carnage, and beyond the immediate destruction the wider fallout would be just as horrifying. Numbers made no sense to his mind. Four of five killed in a bar or a shopping centre sounded shocking, but real. The kind of figures broken by tomorrow's news broadcast would be vast multitudes of that sense. In the thousands, a number to stand with the worst tragedies in history.

Just think of it as war, Dan had said, but that was easy talk, hard action. Innocent lives just wiped out, and by his hand. Because it would be him that would set down the suitcase, him that would get off a stop later, just slipping through a crowd that wouldn't even know of his existence. Not running because that would attract attention, just stepping out as part of the general, lucky exodus, making his way to the surface and then away, quickly away, a car waiting, a driver to take him to the airport. Probably they'd be watching the airports, but it would be a race by then and they couldn't be everywhere.

He'd be away, or they'd take him in. It was as simple as that. And if they took him in he'd have his alibi ready, more than one in fact. They'd question his ticket, where he was going, and probably they'd get rough, knowing his history. But he could handle that, if he so chose. But maybe he wouldn't choose, maybe he'd find solace in confession. Answer, finally, for the things that he had done.

He circled the city for what seemed like hours. On through early morning towards day. He walked around the National Gallery in Leicester Square, wandering through the various wings to gaze without much thought at the Van Gogh's and the French Impressionists, taking in the serenity of Constable and the manic rage of Turner's seascapes, ate a lunch of cod and chips straight from its newspaper wrapping up in Croydon, right in the street, the fish soaked in vinegar, and afterwards found an Irish pub to quench his thirst. But he spoke to no one, and he returned to the safe-house as darkness was falling, spent a sleepless night on the shed floor at the bottom of an ex-priest's garden, some friend or acquaintance of Dan's.

That was the hard part, that night. In the shed, without even the comfort of a sleeping bag, breathing in the earthen stench of damp fungus and potted plants, he did his best not to think of the things that lay ahead. The shadow in the corner was the device, all cased up, all ready for destruction, packed into the discreet shape of a small suitcase. The bomb itself was big, but it was the enclosed space and subterranean aspect of the tunnel that would ensure the utmost chaos, the maximum devastation relying on chain reaction. He lay there on the hard floor, trying to fix on better things, but there were no better things, not in his life. With him, everything was tainted. As it should have been, he supposed.

Sometimes there was almost the offer of an entire alternate existence, but he only caught strands of it; Bríd as his wife, older, and their child – a boy, he knew with absolute certainty. A boy who would know nothing of this, a boy that he would shelter from bigotry and hatred and murderous acts. When he closed his eyes he caught details of them as they could have been, mother and child, heavenly, but it was a difficult thing to bear and so he forced himself awake, sitting up to watch until finally a watery light broke the sky and filtered through the shed window, that small square of glass filthy with cobwebs and dirt.

Not until he was actually on his way did he give room to the idea of disobeying the order. By then he was already in the tube, already standing in the crush of bodies, the suitcase at his feet. It came suddenly, as huge as a punch in the stomach, the thought that he could just get off here with the case, get to the police with it or find some deserted alleyway. Prevent death instead of causing it.

In a way it helped that it would be a difficult thing to do. The easy option now that he had actually come this far was simply to let things run their course, follow the plan as it had been laid down. What had seemed so complicated that only a man of his expertise could be trusted with its execution, now became ridiculously easy.

The tube slowed in preparation for the next stop, and he didn't even have to look up to know that it was time. Just step off, make his way to the surface, the long penitent climb to daylight and the waiting car. But when the doors opened and the crowd parted a little to make exiting room, he gathered up the suitcase.

Now his heart beat hard. There was a time concern, the detonation scheduled for 8:45 a.m., which gave him a little over twenty five minutes, by his estimation. Not long, but maybe long enough.

He searched his mind for the best alternative, but already his body seemed to have decided upon a course. What he would have wanted was to find Dan and to give him back his gift, make him eat it, even. Except, of course, Dan was already gone, back in Belfast since last night, probably, safely surrounded by his closest confidantes and counting down the minutes, the radio on the sideboard already tuned to the BBC in anticipation of the first mention that their mission had been successful. He was safe, untouchable. Just like always.

Without running – because there was a real danger that excessive disturbance could trigger the bomb prematurely – Joe moved steadily south. In truth, it wasn't so difficult. The underground might have been choked with people but the side streets were reasonably clear to a pedestrian, the stores still closed yet. And so, he made it to the river in good time, twenty-five minutes to nine by the distant but readable face of the towering Big Ben.

It crossed his mind that he was betraying everything to which he had sworn allegiance, but in his heart those beliefs that might have swayed him once upon a time were long since dead to him now, and the betrayal, if that was what this really was, made the splash all the more satisfying as he swung the suitcase out over the guard-rail. It arced through the air, hit the surface with a loud slap some ten or fifteen yards out, and there was an instant when he really felt that it would blow. Instead, it began to sink.

He watched until the brackish water had consumed it and then, without looking to see if anyone might have seen him, he turned and walked quickly away. The direction of his retreat was suddenly unimportant, all urgency simply to be elsewhere.

The lunchtime news covered the incident, somewhere below a tremor in Pakistan and the latest in a merry-go-round of talks between Bush and Blair. Joe watched it over a pint of stout in a quiet pub in Portsmouth. He had used the place before, a good town in which to keep a low profile, especially in the winter season when tourists were scarce.

Police were investigating an explosion in the Thames river, right in the heart of London. The newscaster, a dark-skinned woman, into her forties but nice looking, read from a page, and her voice held none of the shock that it could have known, had the circumstances worked out differently. Some damage was reported, part of the banking wall and passing road had experienced some subsidence, and a woman passer-by was taken to hospital with minor injuries after being knocked over by the force of the spraying water. At this time, Scotland Yard were refusing to comment or speculate on the incident, but an unnamed source has indicated that it may have been a failed terrorist attack by a certain Irish Republican splinter group. Security has been tightened at nearby Westminster, thought by many to have been the intended target of the attack.

He watched the television from his seat by the window, along with the other punters who were enjoying a lunch-hour drink. In a casual way, so as not to arouse suspicion, and he watched the news that followed too, even the latest sporting update, the English football team's preparations ahead of the vital World Cup qualifying game away to Spain, and the weather, which promised only more of the same, gale force winds from the east, and rain.

From time to time, he touched his jacket pocket, just to ensure that the money was still there. It was. He had missed his flight, but that didn't matter. He knew how to disappear, even close at hand. There was a time to run and a time to sit tight. Maybe he'd just sit a while. And he had seven thousand pounds in used cash which would be enough to see him through. Not much perhaps in the eyes of many, and small compensation for the part of him that they had taken, but something.

THE WEDDING DAY

The air in Crowley's Bar & Lounge had an intimidating thickness. A wet November Saturday with evening coming in fast, the few gathered guests stood or sat in pockets, chatting in hushed voices so that the conversations wouldn't carry, stopping only to drag at rolled-up cigarettes or to swallow from their glasses. Murphy's for the men, the bulk of the stout broken up by the odd drop of Paddy; sherry for the mothers of the bride and groom; snowballs for the bride and the bridesmaid. The wedding reception was two hours old and had already lost its edge, but they had all been here for wakes too. Celebration or sadness, the atmosphere in Crowley's was always the same.

Snowballs had a way of making Lucy want to cry. She sat with Fiona, her sister, at a table in the centre of the floor and spoke in whispers, keeping her head down. Her eyes studied a peeling beer mat and its spongy dampness was so alluring that she kept wanting to touch it. When she did, the wedding ring looked out of place on her finger, too thick and ugly. Her hands were ugly too, made that way from handling raw meat all week long.

Old Gould, her boss, hadn't wanted to give her the time off for a honeymoon, but then Father O'Leary stopped by and had a word with him and after that everything was okay. Old Gould even called to the church for the service. The butcher shop closed from one to two, so he had the hour to spare. He came up to them at the end of the service, kissed her dryly on the cheek and shook Kevin's hand. 'I hope ye'll be very happy together,' he said, then he had a few words with her father and Kevin's father and hurried away to reopen the shop. He had already given her a wedding present, a pound note folded in with her usual wages. Which, everyone agreed, was very decent of him.

A spurt of laughter rose from the end of the bar, where the fathers of the bride and groom were sitting. John Joe Feehan was a big man, and Kevin was like him in looks, especially around the mouth. They both had the same pinched way of considering things. It made them appear slow where actually they were only cautious. Now that pinched mouth was swallowing a large draught of stout. The paraffin lamp was set at John Joe's elbow and its cast glow made the sweat shine yellow as it traced rivulets down across his bald temples. When he lowered the glass he smiled, a little embarrassed. The bellow of laughter had been his; Lucy's father, Dan, never laughed out loud. It was not his way, even though he had a violent wit. There was no doubt that he had drawn the laughter from the other man, some joke that he'd picked up or a sharp observation shared about someone they both knew.

Lucy watched him but the memory of how he had hit her when she broke the news pushed to the surface, making her lower her eyes to the beer mat on the table and her own red fingers again. The only time that he had ever raised a hand to her, the only time he'd ever raised his voice, even. She deserved it, of course, but it was her mother who had caused him to snap, with her sobbing and nagging and her constant need to end every biting sentence with 'Isn't that right, Dan?' so that he was in the middle of it whether he wanted to be or not, and she got worse and worse until finally he could take no more. Not a slap even, but a punch, and for the better part of a week Lucy felt sure that her cheekbone had been broken. It hurt to eat and to talk, and she couldn't sleep on that side which meant she couldn't sleep at all. Dan had earned himself a reputation for fighting, especially in his younger days, and she'd heard the stories and knew the respect in which he was held by the other men of the village. But all of that was long behind him and it was shocking to everyone when he hit her. She had to tell people that she'd walked into a door. The blow had knocked her to the ground and she saw the look of fear on her father's face as he stood over her. Hannah, her mother, was crying and smiling triumphantly, but when she started to say something about how any girl deserved that for acting like a whore, one glance from Dan was enough to shut her up. Lucy lay there on the floor, crying until something shifted inside of her, or hardened itself to her plight. The following day Dan, ashamed of what he had done, couldn't bring himself to look at her, but he knelt before the fire, trying to coax a blaze, and muttered that she shouldn't worry, that these things happened sometimes and it wasn't the end of the world. She knew he was sorry for hitting her and she wanted to forgive him, so she thanked him in a whisper, and after that the situation was put to rights.

The women stood with Father O'Leary and smiled almost deliriously as they took turns repeating over and over what a happy day this was and what a lovely couple Kevin and Lucy made. 'Kevin's a good lad,' Father O'Leary said, sipping sherry like the two women. 'And Lucy's one of the best. I know they'll be very happy together.'

'Thanks, Father,' Hannah said, and Betty Feehan added that it had been a beautiful service.

'Shame about the rain,' said the priest, 'but at least the farmers will be happy.' No one mentioned the arrangement, because that didn't matter anymore.

At the near end of the bar, Kevin Feehan and his Best Man, Peadar Walsh, were drunk. The gloom was heaviest just here, away from the reach of the paraffin lamp. Peadar was only seventeen, a year younger than Kevin, but nobody made anything of it. They worked together as labourers for Cannon, and before that they'd been in school together. In the two hours of drinking they hardly spoke a word until after the fifth or sixth pint of stout Peadar leaned in and asked, 'What was it like, Kev?'

Kevin thought for a moment and then shrugged.

'Ah come on. Tell us.'

'I don't know what it was like. There didn't seem to be much to it, to tell you the truth. High bloody price to pay, though.'

A nod. 'Ah well. Lucy's a nice girl. You're as well off marrying her as anyone else.'

Kevin wanted to say something in reply to that but the Murphy's made it difficult to think, so he let it go. Down the bar his father was smiling with his eyes closed, the beads of sweat gleaming on his forehead and down his cheeks. Lucy's father was leaning in, sharing something that was obviously a joke or a funny story.

There had been no jokes or smiles that night Dan had called around. Kevin was in the kitchen, scrubbing the day's dirt off his face and arms over a dish of cold water. He heard his father at the door, and the voice of Dan, steady. A moment later, his father's voice rang out. 'Kevin. Come in here.'

No anger, because the decision had already been made. In the living-room, Dan sat in one armchair beside the fire, his father in the other. His mother stood, her face a mask of pained silence.

'Hello, Mr Stack.'

'Kevin.'

John Joe leaned forward, his thick fingers rolling a cigarette by the light of the fire. 'Dan here says his Lucy's expecting.' He put the cigarette to his mouth, then removed it again to pick a thread of Old Holborn tobacco from his tongue. He looked at Kevin. 'What do you know about that?'

The silence was answer enough. Finally, John Joe nodded to himself. 'Well, you'll have to do the right thing, boy, and that's all there is to it. You've made your bed now.'

His mother began to cry, but everyone ignored her.

'I'll go and get that bottle from the cupboard. You sit down here by the fire. We have something to drink to, I think.' John Joe stood with a grunt, his bulk as well as the work he did, furniture removals for Nat Ross, had finally begun taking a toll on his back. As he moved past Kevin he patted his son on the shoulder, and it was a much appreciated gesture, a sharing of strength. Kevin dropped into the armchair by the fire and nodded at Dan. Dan nodded back, and over the whiskey that followed everything was settled.

After a while, the Wedding Cake was cut, a sickly sweet thing baked by Kevin's mother with icing that was oddly greasy. Father O'Leary ate a slice and then excused himself. He had early Mass in the morning, he announced, and really needed to be running along. He shook hands with everyone and wished the bride and groom all the happiness in the world. 'God is smiling on you both,' he said, and they nodded their heads and thanked him.

Hassett, behind the bar, seemed to recognise that the formalities were reaching a conclusion, and he switched on the radio, working the dials until he found music. Something modern filled the bar, a song that nobody recognised, a man's voice. With effort, Dan and Peadar dragged the centre table and the low stools to one side. Kevin and Lucy moved together and began to dance, awkwardly, given the confines of the small flagstone floor. Once, he stepped on the hem of her dress and heard the sound of material tearing, but by then everyone had consumed enough alcohol for that to no longer matter very much.

A second song replaced the first, and this was one that everybody knew: Frank Sinatra singing *Night and Day*. The others paired up, husbands with wives, bridesmaid with best man. They shuffled on the spot for a couple of minutes until that particular duty was done.

'You look lovely,' Kevin said, when the dance was over. The radio was still playing, something unfamiliar again, so he had to lean close. 'Thanks,' said Lucy, and she smiled even though the smell of his breath had a rotten tinge. She remembered that smell from other nights, walking home after dances, when he had kissed her. The stout had something to do with it, his decayed back teeth the rest. They stood awkwardly together in the middle of the floor.

'Well,' he said. 'Another hour and we'll be on the bus.' Fountainstown would be wild at this time of the year, but that didn't matter. Three days by the seaside, time for them to get to know one another, to learn to make the best of things. 'There's long enough for one last drink, I'd say.'

'I'll go in and get changed,' Lucy said. She nodded to Fiona and together they moved across the floor and disappeared into the back room.

Hassett poured more pints. Dan told him to pour whiskeys too, large ones. 'Get that down ya, boy,' he said, laying an arm around his new son-in-law's shoulders. 'You're a good lad. Make sure you do your best by her.' Kevin drank his whiskey and said he would. He'd learned a lot over the past few weeks; he'd grown up. It didn't surprise him anymore that nobody even thought to mention love in any of this. Love was for stories, not for the real world.

THIS IS THE END

Galloway read the letter through, then sat a while and read it again, slowly, digesting every bitter word. It had been just waiting for him, propped against the kettle. Maggie knew him better than anyone else, and she knew enough to leave it where it couldn't be missed. He found it before he even knew that the house was empty. He had picked it up and stared at how his first name, Jack, looked when shaped by her handwriting, while he filled the kettle from the tap and set it on the stove to boil.

As best he could remember, he hadn't felt all that much. Curiosity, perhaps, but certainly not alarm. Most likely, he probably just assumed that she'd decided to spend a few nights at her sister's. Something like that.

While the kettle rumbled towards its boil, he thumbed back the envelope's unsealed flap and pulled out the letter; one of those small lavender-coloured sheets that she always used, even though they cost more than paper should rightly be worth. 'Elegant though,' she said, whenever he complained, and there was no real arguing with that, because they were elegant, if still ridiculously overpriced.

He scanned it as he made his tea, the tea bag straight into his favourite mug, the one with the Newcastle United crest flaked nearly unrecognisable, but he didn't really even begin to take it all in until he was seated at the kitchen table.

Jack, the letter read, *I'm sorry but I've had enough. This is the end.*

And she'd signed it like it really was the end too; Maggie, in a scrawl that probably nobody but him could have made out.

It was nothing like it should have been. In the movies, he would have heard her voice in the words. But that didn't happen. And even trawling over the message, all that he could focus upon was the way she had signed off: just her barely decipherable name. No love, not even best wishes. Hardly a letter at all really, more of a memo or whatever it was that they called those quick note things. He couldn't even begin to realise the implications of it all, but he still felt chilled to the bone by it.

The radio was playing, tuned to that station that she liked, the one that played country music of a morning. He had just come in and switched it on, without thought, and now it was offering up Waylon Jennings and something sort of rockabilly-sounding that turned out to be *Only Daddy That'll Walk The Line.* The day outside was threatening rain, filling the kitchen with a white gloom. He sipped at the tea, glad of its heat, and though it vaguely crossed his mind that things would seem better with a spike or two of whiskey, he settled instead for a couple of spoons of sugar.

None of it made any sense.

A big part of the problem was the lack of a date. It was conceivable that the letter could have sat there for days; he had, after all, been away since Sunday night. That made it nearly a week since he had seen her, and spoken to her, even, because the one time he had tried to call – either Tuesday night or Wednesday, he couldn't be sure – the phone wasn't picked up. At the time, he had just put it down to her stepping out for something, and maybe she had, or maybe she was over with her sister – which was so often the situation that the two of them might as well have been joined at the hip – and he certainly had intended to call back, but what with one thing and another ... Well, no excuses; he should have but didn't, and that was all there was to it.

Everything in the kitchen was in order, but that was no indication of when she might have left. Even the half dozen letters strewn across the floor in the hallway could have been this morning's yield or could have built up over most of the week. It comprised – apart from a quarterly electricity bill – entirely junk mail, of course; a 'You have won a Mi££ion!' lie, and a book club offer of six books for 99 pence being the pick of the litter. He thought about another mug of tea but he was suddenly very tired and to make it seemed too much like work, so he swayed instead towards the easier option of the whiskey bottle so lonely in the drinks cabinet, pouring a water glass halfway full and then putting the bottle's stopper in his pocket so that he wouldn't be tempted to give up too early. Well, that at least was no problem.

The drink helped. It burned going down, but at least that was some kind of sensation, and with the worst of it over he gave the letter another try. *I've had enough. This is the end.* All right, so maybe what they had wasn't exactly Mills & Boon, but who had that, for Christ's sake? He supposed that it couldn't have been easy for her, what with him being away from home so much, but he had to work, didn't he, and she'd have had a different tune to play if he spent his days divided between the pub and the betting shop, like plenty of others around here. She always had money to spend; well, not always, but a sight more than most, including her sister. They had this place, and it was pretty nice. A bit small, maybe, but it was just the two of them, and how much room did they need, anyway? And the area was good too, safe enough to walk to the corner shop of an evening without having to fear for your life. He doubted that she missed the place where she had grown up, a place where even twenty years ago they'd have knifed you for your cigarettes. *This is the end* was pretty melodramatic, but surely she knew when she had a good thing going.

Slowly he worked at the bottle, and it was easy work, knowing that the seal had already been cracked when he got there. Even if he managed to drain the thing – and that, more or less, was the plan – at least he wouldn't have the guilt of knowing that he'd finished out the entire bottle.

She'd left him; that came as the whiskey worked its bitter kind of magic, turning him morose. She'd found someone else and she'd left him in the lurch. What was he, fifty-five? Which made her forty-eight. No spring chicken, and a little hard around the edges, but she was still a handsome-looking woman. He had kept her too goddamned well, that was his mistake. It wasn't just divorced men who had to pay maintenance.

Well, that was fine when he was getting the benefits of it, but now some other dirty bastard was moving in on her.

Even thinking all of this he recognised the edge of the whiskey in the words, the kind of aggression that wasn't really him at all. He indulged in such thoughts a while, sipping at the whiskey, holding onto each mouthful before swallowing so that he could keep the heat for his tongue, but once his mind had exposed them for what they were they lost much of their edge and, really, ceased to matter. Well, if that was what she wanted, to hell with her. What they had going was a thin enough thing these days, and the only times that they collided much any more was after a good night down at the pub when it was that age-old situation, any port in a storm, or else when they argued. And it was the second of these things which dominated. It was doubtful that either of them could have remembered what had drawn them to one another in the first place. Black magic, her sister said. So if she wanted out, he'd not be the one to barricade the door. But if she went, let her remember who was doing the walking. He'd put enough into her; let her fancy man take up the tab from now on, and that included keeping a roof over her head. Because this roof was spoken for.

Actually, her going might not have been a bad thing, as far as he was concerned. He was fifty-five, yeah, but that wasn't over the hill these days, not by a long way. His work kept him well enough, which made him an enticing prospect as far as most around here were concerned. Yeah, there was life in the old dog yet, maybe he could finally get himself a little bit of enjoyment out of the world. Down at the local, he'd seen some of the girls, early twenties and dressed like strip-o-grams, some of them, three or four vodkas and they were anyone's. He could keep them fed with vodka by the bottle. Maybe all of this would turn out to be the best thing that could have happened for him.

Well, enough was enough. He drained his glass and rose unsteadily, took the bottle, now seriously depleted, by the neck and made for the living-room, dropping into his favourite armchair and out of habit reaching for the television's remote control. Thoughts of all the local girls with their low-cut tops and fleshy legs could keep until later;

for now, he had all the company he needed in his whiskey and the television's twenty-eight inches of *Grandstand*. It didn't much matter what sport they were showing. Tired as he was, the rhythms of *Football Focus* and then Davis Cup tennis, interrupted now and again by racing from Northampton, were wonderfully soothing. The whiskey put up no struggle either, and some time after it was gone the stupor was invaded by a creeping sleep.

When he woke, it was late, dark outside, and inside too, apart from the television screen showing something gruesome. He watched it, bleary-eyed and vacant, and though his head was beating like it was about to hatch, he recognised enough of it to know that it was some kind of crime series. Cop shows were heavy on grit, these days. It was supposed to be reality, but who'd want that kind of reality? Everyone believed in crackheads and rapists and paedophiles, but nobody wanted them in their living-rooms of an evening. He punched at the buttons of the remote control, and he had to back up when he realised that *One Foot in the Grave* was on and that he had passed it. Old-fashioned humour. That was what television should always be.

It hurt to move, but eventually thirst overpowered any kind of pain, and he forced himself. Tea was just the ticket. He set the kettle on the stove, bearing the noise of the water rising to the boil as a necessary price to be paid. And while he waited, he slumped down at the kitchen table.

The note was there; his hand had it and his eyes were reading it: *I've had enough. This is the end.*

And the implications of the words bloomed through his head with a suddenness that was jarring. He had to force a breath, wondering how he could possibly have missed this. How he could possibly have seen it any other way?

She was dead. Maggie, his wife of more than thirty years. All right, so they'd had their moments, but he had always worked hard for her, had given her everything he could to make her happy. A nice house, money to spend, the freedom to come and go as she pleased. Well, maybe not that last one, not exactly, but he had never complained much when she went missing for hours at a time to visit her sister. And through it all, there was this thing that he had never noticed, or which he had simply chosen, long ago, to ignore. Grief, he supposed it was, maybe some sort of depression. It had always been just the two of them, no children, and he knew that could upset a woman. But surely she was past all of that, forty-eight was a bit old to be getting broody. Must be that the menopause was kicking in, probably playing havoc with her hormones.

Still, whether it was mostly down to her or not, there was no denying the guilt that he felt over the situation, and the whiskey probably didn't help there either. To think he had been home, what? must be ten, twelve hours anyway, and all he had done after reading the note was to drink himself stupid and crash out in front of the horse racing. And all the while she was lying dead somewhere. Had to be, because if she had been found surely he'd have known about it.

The tea was good against his stirring hangover, and he sipped at it and winced at how hot and sweet it was. His mind was still working at a slow crawl, and it was a minute of radio noise, some generic and forgettable tune, before he began to think of how she might have done it. This at least was something to hang on to, a grizzly subject but a substantial one.

A gun was out of the question. Too messy, for a start,

given her general sense of neatness. Of course, the mess wouldn't be hers to clean up, but still, he couldn't quite see her taking that option. And anyway, how would she get her hands on a gun? All right, so there were backstreet pubs in town where you could find one if the price was right, but Maggie wouldn't know that, wouldn't know where to begin.

No, not a gun, and keeping to the neatness theory, probably not a razor blade or knife either. She wouldn't fancy the pain of that, or the sight of her own blood. She had such a dread fear of injections that she refused to take the yearly hay fever shot, even though she suffered most brutally with pollen. So, ruling those things out, he was still left with the options of a pills overdose, a hanging, or a plunge into the river. None of which was very pleasant but all of which seemed possible. She'd be efficient, whichever way she chose; that much he knew for certain. Of those three, assuming that he wasn't overlooking any other method, the rope would probably leave the least room for failure. With an overdose or with jumping into the river, someone could well happen along in time to intervene. The rope, once she had settled on a quiet enough place – and it must have been quiet, since she obviously hadn't yet been found – would take only a few seconds. If she did it right. If the knot slipped it could have been a slow process, death by strangulation instead of the single brisk snap that would close the door on everything.

It was terrible to think of her like that. She had probably gone out of town, some place she would have known well enough to be sure of the necessary privacy. The Lake District, maybe. They'd rented a caravan there for the last three years and Maggie always did a lot of walking during those holiday weeks. Some quiet spot that she knew; wasn't it entirely possible that such a scouting mission had even been her purpose when she started nagging him to take her there. Said that she'd read about it in a Sunday paper and that it was supposed to be beautiful. Which it was, of course, but thinking about it now, maybe she had been contemplating suicide for years. Planning it, even. Now she was up there, hanging from some tree, and if a few days had passed the birds and some of the other small animals, rats and such, would have been at her. It would be quiet there in the wintertime; even with a search party out looking for her, it could be weeks before they found any trace at all. And by then, Christ only knew if they'd even turn up that much.

His mind played it over, how it might have been. She'd be crying surely, no one could be about to end it all and not shed a tear for the things that they were giving up. It wouldn't be easy for her, climbing a tree and crawling out along a branch to tie up the rope, but she'd be sensible in this as she was in most things, practical, and she'd look for the most suitable tree for the job. Surely she thought of him as she did it, and he actually hoped that she did, and that she felt bad for what she was doing to him, leaving him like this, without a word or even a hint. Well, maybe there had been hints, but she would have known that he was not one to look too closely at things. If she wanted him to know that she was this unhappy, she should have made it clear. Subtlety had never been his strongest suit.

If it had to be, then he hoped that it was quick.

The tea was gone and it was nearly eleven, but having slept most of the day he was no longer tired. He sat there at the table, the fingers of his left hand tapping out a little arpeggio rhythm that rang dull because of the clean white tablecloth. He moved the mug and noticed the wet brown ring it left behind. That would have angered her nearly to screaming at how inconsiderate he could be, but he didn't have to worry about anyone screaming at him any more. He had no one to clean up after him now.

More out of habit than anything else, he gathered his coat and moved to the door, thinking that he'd just make last orders down at the local pub. Just the one, but that would help his hangover no end. He'd leave the girls alone, it wouldn't be right for him to be trying to pick up some skirt, not tonight, not after what had just happened. It wouldn't be such a hardship having to leave all that for a week or two. Give everyone time to hear about it. Tonight he'd indulge his sorrow a little bit, and have a drink, or two at the outside, to her memory. Still though, if sympathy moved some kind heart to offer a comforting embrace, or a shoulder to cry on, well, it wouldn't be polite to refuse now, would it?

He switched off the television set and the living-room was plunged into a better darkness. Soothing, but not so all-encompassing that he had to feel his way along. There was always some residual light to be had in a city house, the vague wash of a nearby street light or leakage from some other home's front porch. He slipped on his coat and moved towards the door but the doorbell brought him to a sudden stop.

It would be nothing, of course; some neighbour probably, perhaps they'd had to sign for a parcel or something from the postman. But his heart was beating hard. No sense to it, but the apprehension was a real enough thing just the same. Could it be the police? Maybe they had found something.

Suddenly he needed that drink, and the company of a packed bar too, all that good light and atmosphere. The doorbell rang again, not the ding-dong variety but one of those that chimed bell-like for as long as you held your finger to the button.

'All right,' he called, not his voice at all, far too dry to be his. 'Just a minute.' Grumbling as though he had been disturbed, but this at least was better, more like it should be. He shrugged free of his coat and folded it roughly over the back of the settee. It would have been better if he had thought to put on the chain, just in case, because you never could tell what kind of people might be wandering the streets at this hour, kids all hopped up on aerosol cans or glue or some such thing. But it was too late for that now.

His hair was tossed and it looked like he had been asleep, which of course he had been. That, at least, would look better if it was the police, better anyway than if he looked as though he were just heading out on the beer.

He fumbled at the lock, snapped it open. With a violent force, the door pushed inward, forcing him back. With all the whiskey inside it was not easy to catch his balance, but somehow he achieved it, after a few steps.

'What's this all about?' he gasped, but the man who filled the doorway didn't answer, maybe hadn't even heard. He just stepped inside and shut the door. The guy wasn't exactly huge in stature, but he was overweight and thickset about the chest and shoulders, and when he switched on the hall light, he was smiling. He had a mean look, of the kind commonly found in the roughest areas of any city, a wide head set on a thick neck, a cap of oily black hair and a face relaxed into folds. His mouth was smiling, a slash of a thing, but no piece of that smile made it to his small staring eyes.

Galloway himself was no hard case, but he wasn't soft either. He may not have been as broad as this guy but he was taller, and he had boxed some in his earlier years and knew how to use the extra inches on a reach. He readied himself for the onslaught, trying to gain the best from his racing heart and wishing that he had paid more heed to his instincts. But it was too late for all of that now.

Slowly he backed into the living-room, hoping that some advantage there might present itself to him. The invader just seemed amused by his efforts at retreat, and he took his weight from the shut door and followed, like this was a game that he had played before.

'You found her note.' There was no shape of a question in the words, nor seemingly much expectation of a reply.

Galloway only stared, but it was enough.

The invader's smile widened, then spurted laughter. Just a moment of it, and then it fell away and he wiped a big hand over his mouth. 'I'm sorry,' he said, sounding sincere even though he was smiling still. 'I'm not laughing at you. It's only the situation, it never changes. Little details maybe, but really everything is much the same as always.'

'What the hell are you talking about?' Galloway whispered.

'You've taken a few drinks, am I right? You found the note and then hit the bottle. That's what we were counting on really; I wasn't so sure, but your wife knew that you wouldn't let us down. You found the note, and which was first? That she'd left you or that she'd done herself in?'

Galloway was stunned. He swallowed hard and answered, though he didn't much want to. 'That she left me.'

The invader laughed again and nodded. 'That's about right too, I guess. Guys like you always think that first. You were probably halfway down the bottle before the other thought even crossed your mind. Am I right? Huh? Well, you don't have to answer that if you don't feel like it, I think I already know the answer anyway.'

'You mean she's not dead?'

'No, she's alive and kicking, pal.'

'So she *has* left me.' Anger came now, frothing to the surface. 'I'd have given her more credit than to think she'd have teamed up with the likes of you though.'

'Why don't you take it a tad easy on the insults, I'm just trying to explain the situation as best I can. All right? And the fact is, she hasn't left you. I'm afraid that it's you who'll be doing the leaving.'

Now it was Galloway's turn to laugh. The whiskey had taken flame and it was beginning to melt away his earlier fear. He'd take a beating if that was what was needed, but maybe he'd have it in him to dish one out too. 'You've got a real good sense of humour there, mister. I'm going nowhere.'

The invader shrugged, like it didn't matter much to him either way. Or like it had already been decided and the subject was no longer open to argument.

'Why don't you read the note again, pal,' he said, nodding with his head towards the kitchen table, where the note lay. 'Your wife told me to tell you that it's all in there.'

'I've already read the note,' Galloway said, but he was getting the cold feeling again. He crossed the room to the open kitchen and snatched up the letter, his fingers working to smooth out the creases.

Jack,
I'm sorry but I've had enough. This is the end.
Maggie

The invader stood there, arms folded across his big chest, watching Galloway read, waiting for the message to sink in. When a minute passed and it wasn't happening, he cleared his throat. Galloway looked up, like a man rising from a dream.

'What she's saying pal is that she's had enough of you. The marriage is over, but it's you who is going, not her.'

Then he reached inside his coat and produced a gun, the barrel lengthened by a silencer already attached. He just held it, not pointed at anything in particular, as though he had surprised even himself with such sleight of hand.

'Wait,' Galloway said, and he held his hands out in some kind of useless reflex gesture.

The invader looked at him and there was nothing in his face, nothing to say whether he would wait or would choose to act, nothing at all but that same slash of smile.

'I'll leave. There's no need for any of this. I'll just go. She can have it all.'

'She'll have it all anyway, Jack. Widows always do.'

The first shot sent Jack Galloway stumbling backwards against the counter top. His shirt was a mess and it hurt where the heat of the bullet had fused the cotton to the flesh. He clutched at the wound. Blood seeped between his fingers, a red that was nearly black, not like the films at all, and one fingertip pressed into the torn flesh and touched the splintered rib.

He felt the edge of the counter against his back and the stainless steel of the sink cold against the touch of one reaching hand. The invader was moving towards him from the living-room. All that mattered suddenly was to be away, but the best that he could do was turn his back. Now it hurt to breathe, like there wasn't enough air in the world, and he gritted his teeth and forced each lungful, telling himself over and over that it would be okay. Telling himself this even when the second shot came, the sound of it whining because of that silencer, and the impact like a punch between his shoulder blades.

Whispering it, assuring himself, even as he slipped slowly towards the floor, that second shot bringing the real coldness, the end coldness.

But as it was he didn't have to wait, because bracing himself against the touch of the shadow, he never felt the third and final shot.

'This is the end,' he might have said, if he could have spoken. 'I've had enough.'

Really though, the time for such words was past.

A BLUE NOTE

Some years ago, I found myself in a room downtown watching him shoot up. I can't say with any degree of certainty whether or not it was his first time doing it, because even though we were as close as two people could ever be we tried hard not to live in one another's pockets too much, but I remember that he did show an amount of innocence where the needle was concerned, how he scratched a soft white line up the inner flesh of his forearm but seemed to freeze when he reached the bluish lump of vein just where he opened his elbow. It may have been his first time tasting the smackshot or maybe he was simply afraid of the needle, just as a great many junkies tend to be. It's that tenuous balance between terror and addiction. Someone else had to do the honours that day, or that night, because days and nights seemed very much like two halves of the same trick back then, and there were always windows painted black and some bare lightbulb burning eighty white hot watts, a peeling glare that just as much as the drugs and all the rest added to the sense of unreality of that time.

He was destined for something more, everyone could see it. I had *always* seen it, and told him so as often as he needed. It was Coltrane all over again, all those self-destructive musical prayers, except that this was no derivative, no mimic. This was taking up a saxophone and blowing until nothing else mattered because there *was* nothing else, no ends and no beginnings, just the melodies that he scraped from the air, godly things already, and then turned them from the perfectly mediocre to the ridiculously sublime. People had already begun to call him Jake by then, all that new crowd that had filtered in, hungry on the promise of the best kinds of highs. Jake Renshaw, because it was agreed that was a name to carry more weight than Jackie. He didn't understand it and neither did I, but he became two people just around then, and the old him, the real him, increasingly became a face for only me to see. Apart from his minutes on the stage, he was an actor playing a role.

I remember how he shot up on the living-room floor that day or night, a girl who seemed just then like she was all that and more helping the needle on when his flesh or his fingers flinched in last resistance. She had the kind of smile that was at once dirty and hungry, a bedtime smile made sour by her flashing eyes and leering teeth. Everyone wanted some of it, and she was ready to give. I remember, vaguely, that there had been more than enough to go round. He lay there gasping while the needle jogged in time to his racing pulse, hanging from his vein like a starving leech. After it had fixed him up he'd leaned back against the seat cushions of the couch, closed his eyes and clenched his teeth in a manic, agonised way, a skeletal gag that would come to mark him after he'd lost all that weight and after enough bad living had begun to rot away not just his lips but his cheeks as well. Back then though, the lows were still off in the distance, and we all knew of them but no one quite believed. They were stories for a campfire, and we told ourselves that we were different, that we could handle it. We believed that money made all the difference.

He had money. Generous to a fault, it came and went like a visiting cousin with him, and I know for certain that he was ripped off plenty of times, but he never cared about that, as long as there was enough to get by. In the beginning, it was only the music that really mattered, and not even the studio stuff or the big gigs but the dropping by unexpectedly to one of the small down-at-heel nightclubs that in the old days lay scattered all across the West Side. Just slipping in, noticed only by the doorman who smilingly took a five and nodded a conspiratorial silence, and then almost drowning in that darkness until a second or maybe a third shot of rye grounded him enough so that he could ease his way to the front. And, when the opportunity presented itself, he'd use the lull to climb up on the small bandstand, screw on his mouthpiece, bow his head and just begin to play.

That was where he mattered most, up on stage in a small club, made pale from the milky spotlight, caressing riffs to fruition through a variety of ruffled time signatures. Taking Parker for a walk, he muttered once, not even into a microphone but to the bass player maybe, or to himself, and then he closed his eyes again. That's what it was, taking old things and making them impossibly new, or grabbing hold of them and twisting in ways that nobody else could even conceive of doing. And if the peaks were enough to kill the breath in your throat then the furrows had all the impact of a kick in the stomach. Even if you didn't know his story you couldn't fail to know that this was a man struggling with demons, a man who lived by the hour, and who carried around with him a pain that was worse than anything the physical could ever bestow. I know his story because I lived it with him, but it is all just a mess of facts that don't really begin to make up the full picture. Just think about the worst things you can, the greatest kind of sufferings that a child can know and still somehow endure, and you'll begin to get some idea of who he was. Listen to his music, and you'll understand him.

At first it was a joyride. We'd been through everything and now the world was paying us back. At least, that was how it felt. I did the little things, carried his bags, drove him where he needed to go, found us the very finest reefer and also the kind of women who could keep a party alive even after everyone else had gone home. I watched over him; we were brothers in every way imaginable, and I loved to listen to him play because I could always tell when he was playing to me.

The best nights have lived on as dreams. We had a time in Paris, one of our best, just a basement club with no stage, half a dozen rows of pews salvaged from some demolished church, their ancient woodworm-speckled oak shining in the room's randomly placed wall lamps. Everyone brought their own wine and a small, foolish line formed for a turn with the corkscrew. The hardened patrons could be recognised by their overcoats bulging in odd places with further concealed bottles and by the little smirks that said this would be a long night and they knew it, they were ready for it. We all drank straight, no formalities here, no such French need for glasses or decorum, and it seemed easier then somehow to understand what was important and what wasn't. Miles Davis stood there beside my brother in that little open wedge of floor, waiting his turn and nodding his head to the slow, taunting beat of a solo that made obsolete everything that had gone before and which sounded a closing note on the proceedings because by the end of it there was nothing left to say, nowhere left to go. There were tears in Miles' eyes, but my brother's face was streaked with them, and it was impossible to resist the lure of the melody he found and settled on in among his jabbing riffs. The music ached, and we ached with it. That 3 or 4 a.m., Paris had unearthed another grand work of art. Afterwards, I embraced him and there was no need for either of us to say that we had shared a moment of perfection, the kind of moment that even a genius will stumble across only three or four times in his life, if he is constantly active and is also blessed with the luck of many, many years good health and inspiration. There were other nights and other highs, but that Paris basement was a definite peak, and then the heroin reached the scene and after that everything felt compromised.

The truth of it is that after the light went out the rest was hard to bear. The first gig he missed was really the end of the road, though we struggled along for a while after it, fighting, loving and hating. Too close, the obvious concealed itself from my eyes, and then one morning I awoke alone in a strange bed. There was noise in the kitchen, the soft clanging of plates being readied for breakfast but I seemed to wake a little too fully because the realisation of everything hit at once. I stood under the shower, less to wash than to cry. After that it was all just waiting and counting down. Jackie died probably two years before his heart finally stopped beating. He died the moment that the drugs made him walk and talk, and that was the same moment that the music lost its focus. His fingers could still find the right notes for a while, and only those of us who knew him well knew that his playing had lost its passion. To the watching eye, the addiction appeared slow in rotting him away, but it was brutal in its treatment of the soul and that was the real end, not just the beginning of it.

I lived through him, and now he is gone but I am still living. We were not so different, Jackie and I, except where talent was concerned. In the end, I think it was the talent that proved a curse, that caused his undoing. But maybe the temporal brilliance of that exploding spark was worth the inevitable burnout. All I know is that I live a half-life without my brother now, but I am thankful to him even for granting me that much, because were it not for his strength, his ability to take on all the suffering that came at us and bottle it up to exploit in different later ways, I would not have survived. He was my example then, and still is even now. With his passing, the world has lost its vigour, and not just for me. I see it everywhere I look; on the subway, in the streets and bars. People are existing, nothing more, the colours have been drained from the world. I get by because I have something they don't have, the memories that crowd my dreams, and that makes me the lucky one, even though the memories that come are so blue and so laced with anguish that I can do nothing but bow my head and cry, or pray for these moments to pass and better, brighter ones to come.

THE DYING BREED

He was just another old man back when I knew him, washed out and holding up one corner of Mac's bar, fishing for drinks. Jack. Whiskey was his poison, and if I was flushed I'd help him out, but mostly he had to make do with beer, just like the rest of us.

'Kid,' he'd say; just that, his effort at gratitude without giving away too much ground, and he'd swallow from his glass, fighting to take his time. His voice had no music left in it at all. He called everyone Kid, everyone who stood him a drink, at least, and I doubt that he could tell us apart, one from the other.

We all knew who he had once been, back in a better life. Those were days long since gone, but the past dies pretty slowly for some men, especially in places where nothing much happens any more, and sometimes, when his sober edge had dulled, he'd get to talking. Chewing his tongue, the stories scraping free, telling about the old days.

Words made sick with what went unsaid, and if the snatches of memory were windows on to his life, then they were also badly recalled and rarely knew any kind of satisfactory resolution. He'd talk, but in spurts, and then his rheumy eyes would lose their focus and the words always fell away to nothing. After a while he'd flail a trembling hand for the solace of his glass, needing it suddenly like breath.

That was the 1930s, the cusp of everything. America's real turn of the century; forget what the calendars say. Civilisation had finally taken hold, and the Depression, which had broken many a farmer's heart, was beginning to ease its grip. The future looked bright.

They wrote about Jack, though in the pages he was always Jack Beam. 5'7', lean as a post, hard as bedrock. History books designed to chart the west devoted entire chapters to his life, or the slice of his life that counted for anything in their eyes, and they recalled in glamorous hand his various exploits, painting them from the desperate to the spectacular. I knew the myth and I knew the man, and I guess the truth was some lost place in between.

He ranked with the best of them, though; that much is for certain. A hard man who did bad things for all kinds of reasons and, occasionally, for no reason at all. At times, an outlaw hunted down and almost hung; at other times still, a hero. But, for good or bad, he was one of those who helped to tame the wild country.

There was law around here by the 1930s; with society came rules. The sheriff's department accommodated him when he needed a cell for the night, and even allowed him to continue carrying his gun, a battered old Colt revolver that looked like nothing but had done for plenty in its time. Mostly though, they tended to leave him alone.

He wore that gun in the old way too, slung low on his left hip, tanned leather holster bound to his thigh with a rawhide thread. I had seen that gun up close, had even handled it. The iron of the barrel was a brackish shade of grey, and the frail-grained sandalwood butt set a roughness through the pale, sweaty veneer of varnish. In all the years I knew Jack, I longed to see him draw the thing, but the one time he did, I missed it.

The lawmen tolerated him, really, because he had become something of an attraction, and the town council recognised his intrinsic worth. Enough time had passed, it seemed, for the West to take on certain nostalgic hues, and both the romantics and the commercially minded were hungry to start creating myths and capitalising financially from their work. Jack Beam was an ideal character, of a value with Billy the Kid, Jesse James and Doc Holliday, but what raised him above those legendary outlaws was that he had beaten the odds. He had seen and done it all, and survived. Now, he was the last of his kind; a dying breed.

People came from everywhere, tourists willing to spend their hard-earned dollars on booze and dinner and maybe a couple of nights in some overpriced cat-house posing as a fancy hotel. They came, the stern middle-aged women with asses built for sitting, and the scrawny fellows from back East, all neatly shaven except for little toothbrush moustaches and decked out in stupid candy-striped shirts and the latest fashion of wire glasses, and I'd hear them muttering amongst themselves that the old boy didn't really look so tough, just another decrepit drunk, nothing at all like the stories said. But they'd watch him anyway, as they would with animals in a zoo. Jack sat there with nothing to his name but his nearly empty glass and his memories of shining days and things debased, and I'd hope he couldn't hear the talk that I was hearing.

He was slow with everything by the end, except with putting down the whiskey. That was a skill he never lost. It never so much as cracked a smile on him either, though he wasn't built for smiling much, it has to be said. It did make him unsteady, but he was unsteady in many ways, by then.

The scrape that peppered his voice was put there from a bullet, marked by a fold that didn't sit quite right down in the leathery jowls of his throat.

After about the twentieth time of asking, he told me that it happened down in Del Rio. He'd been working as a hired gun, during a land feud. Just like in the books, except that the books talked about a lot of rights and wrongs, and down there it was about greed, and nothing much else.

Spare with words, but still so full of colour:

'Riggs, the feller's name was that hired me on. Kilt men for him, more than he was worth. More too than the fifty dollars I took for doin' it.'

The stories liked to talk in numbers, but Jack never offered a yield. Dead men should be worth more than a notch on a gun; that was something he said once, and I guess it stuck with me.

He sunk the stub of an index finger into the hollow, and winced, probably with remembered pain.

'Got me this in a bar down there. I was drinkin' and a gun went off over a game of cards. I took the stone for it, hit me like the kick of a mule. Only time I ever been shot, and the bullet wasn't even meant for me. Every time I swallowed, there was a taste of lead. I thought that was it, for sure.

'Anyhow, I kilt me the man what done it and rode for the border. Made it a ways but fell short of Mexico. Doc in some small place cut the bullet out, talkin' 'bout how if it'd been an inch either way I'd a had it, that it was the devil's luck really. Guess it just wasn't my time. Took months 'fore it healed enough to let me talk again, and I ain't never been right with words since.

'I carried the bullet around with me for a time, like for a souvenir, but then I done gone and lost the thing. At night though, I can still feel it. Like a boot heel, pressin' down, chokin' me.'

Time contrived against him, years spent a certain way, laid out on hard trails and on the wrong kind of women. But there was something that set him apart from everyone else I ever met, a strength that revealed itself in small ways even through the feeble body and the increasing creep of senility.

His face was thickset, stubborn around the white tufted brows and the cleaved line of jaw. He shaved, but not often; saw it as a dalliance, and said so. For an old man he wore his hair too long, but it was thin and losing colour and fell where it would without mattering much. He looked nothing like the pictures in the books, but his was a face that could finish the stories his mouth began. And sometimes, when he rose from the shadows to hit the day just right, that face could take on the merest hint of the way it used to be.

I knew little about Jack beyond the stories, but listening to him brought a modicum of understanding. The legend smothered him, but it was a coat, not really the essence of the man, at all. When he talked, what came through above everything else was the strength.

Beyond everything, dignity prevailed, and when death finally came, it seemed fitting that he fell to the very thing which had tamed the west. I wasn't there to see it but plenty were, and they say he stood right in the road, drawing that old Colt just a heartbeat too late on the car that ran him down.

ALL THAT GLITTERS

That evening, our last together, my father cracked open a bottle of good whiskey. The room was dark except for the red glow of a settled fire in the hearth and the shadowy outpouring of a candle's still leaf of flame from its place on the sideboard. Trying to ignore the tension in the house, I sat in my usual place, the armchair by the fire, and watched the ash smoulder rather than have to see him move about. He set the bottle on the small dining table and its cumbersome sound made me picture in my mind the glass butt ringing the scratched oak beneath the dirty tablecloth. Then he mumbled something about glasses and moved into the kitchen, taking on his back my noncommittally offered, 'Hmm'.

His chair was opposite mine. He returned, the rubber soles of his boots smacking out damp notes on the flagstone floor, and I had to turn to take the offered glass. It felt small and shapely in my hand and I held it raised for him to fill. For the moment, though, I was ignored as he hauled his chair closer – it squealed like filed nails with the movement – and dropped heavily into its embrace. I heard the rim of his glass sing against the bottle's lip and the soft river sound of the pouring whiskey. He cleared his throat and leaned forward until he was touched by the fire's glow.

'Here.'

He passed me the bottle and I took it, having to lean awkwardly forward myself. I nodded thanks and filled my own glass. It splashed from the bottle, making the sound of gasping breath and a drop escaped onto the soft curved pad of flesh between my thumb and index finger and ran up my sleeve. I wanted to slump back into my chair and raise the wetness to my mouth but my father continued to hold his forward crouch so I did too.

I sipped whiskey; he just cradled the little glass tumbler in his big right hand. I stole glances at him and his face wore the split mask of shadow and light. The fire snapped out a spark and he used it as an excuse to give it his attention. He set the glass on the floor between his feet, picked up the dusty poker from the kerb and began to disturb the contented orange of the smouldering coals. The half block of beech shifted, revealing a charred ashen underside. Sleeping flames began to spout, licking to appease their risen hunger.

You won't talk me out of it, Da. I'm going and that's it. Words that, though unspoken yet, tasted sour in my mouth, even with the persistent intake of the whiskey. But I needed them, and I knew that I would have to use them. He would try something, some plea, threat or blackmail, some play for sympathy, and I would be glad of the words then.

'Mooney bought himself a motor car yesterday,' was all he said.

I held the glass to my mouth, and paused. In that pause the distilled scent floated from the spirit in tendrils of clear smoke or steam and filled my mind. In slow degrees, my shoulders relaxed and I realised that I had been tensed for one more argument. 'What kind of motor car?' I asked instead, and wondered if he picked up the tremolo that edged my words.

His mouth twisted in the firelight, a gesture familiar except for the shadows. 'Don't know. A motor car, that's all Cannice Crane in the village said.'

'New?'

'I suppose so.' He put down the poker, giving the fire back its peace, and picked up his glass. Still, he did not drink.

'Must've cost him a quare penny, that.'

'Hmm.'

It was our last night together, maybe the last time we would ever see one other again. In the morning I was leaving for Dublin and the ferry to England. I knew what he felt about it but I knew what I felt, too. He was an old man, and the land was a dead thing these days. I would be thirty in May, and if I went now, there was still a chance for me. Maybe. I had dreams about America.

He drank at last, a big swallow that he held in his bloated cheeks for a long moment. His eyes clenched shut as the burning whiskey took the jerking walk down into his stomach, then he gasped the dark air and raised his glass to me. 'Health,' he said, belatedly.

I nodded, raising my own glass. A span of darkness hung between his and mine but there was no attempt at reconciliation. 'Health,' I murmured, echoing my father. I had heard him use the salute so often; Christmases, Sunday nights, a hundred or a thousand unnameable other times, marking some event whose details were vague or insignificant enough to be forgotten. 'Health.' Just that; not good or bad. It made me think about my mother, many years gone, a part of the overgrown earth down in St Stephen's graveyard in the village. There with the sister I had seen only as a blueness through a grey, threadbare bed sheet and in my mind, in the darkness, can see still.

He was seventy, but old. In the fire's hue, the creases seemed etched in rock, caressing his forehead, cheeks and mouth. His eyes looked heavy and his hair fell in fragile, wispy turmoil, its snowy whiteness burned orange again only by the stolen reflection. It was this place that made you look like that; out in the fields through the blue from grey to dusky grey with the westerly ocean wind beating hardness into your back and shoulders and the low seething sky that brought rain and nothing more until all the world but rock was green, lush with nourishment, and you, finally broken, learned compliance. You lived for the dark loamy earth and the sustenance that it let you draw, and your spirit lived only in the bottom of a bottle. He was all those things. Not *just* all those things, but certainly those things, too.

I drained my glass and felt the loss when the last drops were consumed. He watched me, reaching for the bottle to fill me up again, but I waved him away. 'No,' I said, putting my hand palm-down across my tumbler's yawning mouth. 'I've an early start in the morning.' But I didn't rise and he knew that he could tempt me.

'Have one more,' he said, and I thought about it and shrugged. This time he poured.

I sipped at the refreshed heat. 'You can't talk me out of it,' I said. A part of me felt a twinge of hurt that I could be wrong, that he wasn't even going to try, but I was tired.

He just stared at the spirit in his glass. I sipped from mine.

'If I can't I can't,' he said, at last. 'When I was a boy,

younger than you are now, I wanted to go to London.' He had never told me this. To me, he had always been old.

'Really?' I sat up straight from my crouch.

He nodded, doing that folding thing with his mouth that he always did. 'Word had it that there was plenty of work to be found out there and plenty of money to be made, and it was all we had to do here just to put a few spuds or a bite of bread on the table. I was great with a fella from over Ballinure way, name of Shine. We were supposed to go together.' He turned his eyes to the fire. It had burned itself out now, except for the colour. 'Stupid,' he whispered, so low I hardly heard, and he finished the second half of his whiskey as he had the first.

'What happened?' I asked, suddenly, at this eleventh hour, needing to know.

'I was suited to the soil. And whether you know it or not, so are you, boy.' He met my stare and his mouth formed a crinkled smile. 'Don't worry, I'm not trying to persuade you. I just wanted to tell you something about me. I might not get the chance again.'

I thought of arguing, of saying, *Don't be stupid Da, there's years in you yet*, but I didn't because we would both have recognised empty words.

'My father said not to go. 'They won't thank you for it, Jimmeen,' he said, but I thought different. He was right and I was wrong ...'

Slowly, it dawned on me. 'You went?'

'I did.'

'How was it?'

He looked at me, the firelight dancing veils across his face. 'Home was better.'

We had never been so close, we who had shared the

cramped rooms beneath the thatch all my life as a family and close to twenty four years, just the two of us. And I was never so troubled as I felt at that moment.

I stood in the doorway as the dawn broke across the fields. It was a good sky and the land had the bleached, earthen bronze of summer. The smell of silage filled the air. I spat saliva into the daffodils, convinced that it had taken on the sweet tang, but even in my dry mouth the taste lingered. A cuckoo called out from the sycamores at the roadside and in vain I searched for a hint of something light in the soft green foliage.

This is it, I told myself. *This is the last time you'll see it like this.* Never again would I taste this silage smell or see Slievebaun, that far white mountain, wear the shellac-tinged low horizon cloud in exactly this way. I might return, I told myself, and it might be like this again. Maybe the old man will die on a day like today. But I knew that my eyes by then would be the eyes of a stranger and I would see only the things that I could see and not the things I knew. I would be leaving behind the ghosts, and without me they would no longer exist.

I wanted to be away without the pain of a scene. But when I came inside for my packed bag, my father was there, sitting in his chair by the fire. It was a black hole now, full of last night's spent embers. 'Take care of yourself, boy,' he said, not getting up. His voice was leaden, inert. Clear white light poured through the window and across most of the floor.

'You too,' I said, my throat aching against the sudden swell of homesickness.

'You know where home is if you ever change your mind.'

I nodded, watching the light give brightness to the dust between the floor's flags. 'I'll write,' I said, meaning it at that moment.

'Good.' He gripped the chair's arms and with a grunt pushed himself up onto his feet. 'I'll walk you to the gate.'

'There's no need,' I said but he waved my words away.

'I want to,' he said, so he did.

We shook hands, an awkward gesture but less awkward than a hug. 'England's a hard place for the Irish,' he said, watching the sky for the threat of rain. There was none.

'Don't stay there too long.'

''Tis America I'm heading for,' I said. 'Soon as I can work up my fare.'

The sun had cleared the horizon and found its own part of the sky. Its touch brought the green and the brown to life. My father nodded. In the distant west the Atlantic burned, stung yellow by the bright late dawn light. 'All that glitters is not gold,' he said.

I thought about it. 'I know,' I said, but really I didn't. Not then.

We shook hands again and I turned and started up the road. I was trying to remember everything just as it was at that moment: the gravel road; the overgrown dikes; the sweep and sway of the roadside trees; the ropey briars and the pretty yellow knots of dandelion. I didn't look back, though in my mind I could see him clearly at the gate, wondering what he would do now. I wondered that, too.

IN THE EYES OF THE LAW

'Would you like another drink?' Anna asked. She was standing there holding the bottle that she'd opened specially, the bottle Dan had brought with him. He wished that she'd smile more, but he understood why she didn't. He felt cold inside just now, but she probably felt that way all the time. The glass, cradled in his hands, was still half-full, but he raised it to his mouth, drank deeply, and then held it out for a refill. He watched her while she poured, noticing how the blue and green tangle of veins lay swollen very close to the surface of her pale skin. Her upper teeth pinched little dimples into her lower lip. So serious.

It was Sunday, lunchtime, and if a man couldn't take a little whiskey on a Sunday then when could he take it?

'I'm sorry for calling so early,' he said. 'Did I wake you?'

She shook her head, but he wasn't sure whether that was an answer or a dismissal to his question. She poured herself a drink, barely wetting the bottom of the glass, took a sip and then moved to the armchair opposite. She set the glass down on the small coffee table and seemed to forget all about it.

'You've been thinking about him again,' she said.

'Yeah.'

The house kept a leaden silence; outside, rain threatened,

a February gloom fixed as though it owned the day. Cold, bleak light filtered through the bare branches of the garden willow and shifted with the breeze. He remembered that she had once described this kind of day as weather for tears.

'How's work?' she asked, crossing her legs and then meticulously rearranging her navy skirt around her knees. Her fingers toyed with the hem in a way that made her seem younger than thirty-five, and more innocent than she was.

Dan sighed. 'It's not so bad. They've all stopped fussing over me, at least, even though I know they're still thinking about what happened. Even Wiley, that's my partner. He talks all day, about hurling matches, mostly, but I know what's really on his mind is whether or not what happened was an accident.'

Anna was so thin. Seeing her in this light she looked frail and vulnerable, like some timid orphaned animal cub, and even though he knew her to be strong, the part of him that was a little bit in love with her stirred awake again. Stupid, of course, they both being what they were. Her small feet were bare and her toenails glistened with the cerise pink polish that she had applied because she knew he liked her to wear it.

'You look tired,' she said.

'I've not been sleeping much.' Even his words sounded weary, full of sighs. 'An hour or so and then I'm back there again, on that filthy tenement landing, and I can feel the weight of his thumbs trying to press my eyes back into my head. I wake sweating, and that's me done for the night. On the plus side, I've caught up with a lot of reading these past few weeks.' He tried to smile but it didn't quite fit.

She brought him the bottle again, but this time she

stood beside him while he drank. He looked up at her and understood, and he went obediently at the whiskey, hungry for a piece of its fire. When he was finished she took the glass, then reached for his hand and led him through to the back of the ground-floor apartment. To the bedroom, even though he knew the way.

Inside, music was already playing, the stereo system that he had given her for Christmas spinning a budget-priced jazz CD in shuffle mode. Dan recognised the sax of Coltrane, but not the tune. He sat on the edge of the bed, breathing the musty air of too many hoarded paperback novels through the stinging aftertaste of the whiskey, and watched as she unbuttoned her blouse and then slipped from her skirt. Not much daylight made it back here, and what little did today gave the room a cavernous sense and stripped away the details. When she folded herself into his arms he wished that he could have felt her body tremble even a little, just once, just to make this time different from all the others. But he had already learned the hard way that wishes don't come true, not for the likes of him, and what followed was what always followed, comforting in a fleshy sort of way but inevitably hollow, and the least intimate part of their relationship, if relationship wasn't too strong or too ridiculous a word for what they had together.

When he closed his eyes and let the jazz flow through him he could almost feel himself drifting away. But this was how it was lately, where he could go as much as an hour at a time before his mind hauled itself back to the night that had changed everything for him. During the first days and nights immediately after, he had struggled with an overwhelming urge to vomit, as though his body was trying to purge itself of the memory, but that need had gradually passed and now all he felt was a coldness. Even beneath the cotton sheets, with the weight of a red wool blanket heavy above him and with Anna's naked, sweat-soaked body pressed close, her skin clammy and good against his own, there was still a place for that coldness.

'The small things are so clear, you know,' he said, talking mostly to the ceiling. A frail, abandoned rope of cobweb swayed to the push of some draught. His voice felt so small, not really his at all, made that way from pain. 'It was a cold night, and raining pretty hard. The kind of nights we hold onto our mounds of paperwork for. No one wanted to make the bust. But I'd insisted. I had it rock solid from an informant who had never before steered me wrong that a good amount of the city's crack was moving in and out of there, and I'd spent most of the evening running around trying to get a warrant. That was too much groundwork to write off just because of a little rain.'

Anna kissed his shoulder, but she didn't speak, didn't want to break the flow. They'd only gotten part-way through but that had been enough for him today, so it was enough for her, too.

'I was on the landing when he just appeared in front of me. If I had only let him go past me everything would have been okay. He'd come from the bathroom, had been dumping the stuff, and was trying to make the stairs. They always try to dump it but they never do it right. We found traces of the junk everywhere, the walls, the floor, coating the bowl. Enough to put him and everyone else in the building away for a long time. He was so strung out he hadn't even thought to flush. Tommy Quillan. He was well known to us as a dealer and an addict, a nasty piece of work actually, and if I had just stepped aside and given him a way out we'd have picked him up in a couple of hours or so in one of the city squats and there'd have been no trouble at all. I don't know what I was thinking.'

'You did what you thought was right,' Anna whispered. 'It was your job to stop him.'

His face twisted with a sneer of disgust. 'Yeah, that's me, all right. Detective Sergeant Dan Hennessy, diligent to the last.' Her arm had crept across his chest and felt good there. He needed the embrace. He closed his eyes and there was nothing again but the jazz, something soft and trumpet-driven now. But in that sleepy beat of darkness he found himself waiting once more for the hurtle of a charging body, and even braced against the impact it boasted enough weight and momentum to knock the wind from his lungs, to send him staggering back against the landing wall. They moved together in a hateful tango with Quillan leading but with Dan at fault because he was holding on, clenching fist-fuls of the other man's shirt. The wall stopped everything, its plaster damp and smeared in mould against his cheek. He could hear Quillan's gasps, full of the panic only to be away. And then a sort of understand began to dawn, and hands were on his face, ragged dirty nails biting into the flesh of his cheeks, the heavy pads of thumbs reaching for and then pressing down onto his clenched eyelids. That darkness had been compromised by the blood-pressure blooms of rain-bow streaks and psychedelic bursts, those mad colour inva-sions, and a burning pain raced through his head. He could feel his own hands finding and squeezing the bare bones of wrists, desperate to relieve the pressure of those thumbs, and then he drew his left knee up hard, again and again, knowing by instinct that he was finding the groin area. The weight upon him grew momentarily intense and a grunt of shock and pain rumbled so close to his ear that it might almost have been inside his head. In desperation he pushed against the weight and felt it slip away.

'Everyone was careful not to accuse me of anything. They left me offer up the details, not rushing me. We all know how it is: what you say is what goes down on the book, so think it through before you speak. Someone called for two ambulances, even though one would have done. My eyes were swollen shut, I couldn't see anything but shadows for a couple of hours, and I needed six stitches to a gash on my cheek.'

Evening set in early, given the gloom of the day. Anna slipped from the bed to make coffee. Dan lay there and imagined her standing naked in the dusky kitchenette, her fingertips drumming something complicated on the countertop while she waited for the kettle to boil. All she had was instant, she said, but Dan had told her that was fine, just be sure to stiffen it with a good slop of whiskey. These were the moments that felt cosy, when other things didn't intrude, and they tended to make up for a lot of the hurt. He sat up and took the coffee. She'd been generous with the spike, knowing that he needed it. She perched on the end of the bed, wrapping herself in a lemon-coloured flannel dressing gown. Her peroxide-dyed hair was down, its mousy roots showing darkly through. He liked that, it made him feel as though they were sharing a secret.

'What will the enquiry find?' she asked.

He shrugged. 'Justifiable self-defence. Quillan came at me. It'd be more straightforward if there had been a witness, but the others were securing the rooms downstairs. Still, everyone's saying that the outcome is a formality. One way or another, I'll know by Tuesday. And I've got the medical reports, so ...'

'Will there be any permanent damage? To your eyes, I mean.'

'They're saying no, but that it could take a couple more months before I get back the full sight in my left eye. They didn't tell me until I went back to get the stitches out that I was lucky not to lose it. The retina had been badly scratched, and the pressure had caused a small puncture to the top of the eyeball.'

He took her hand and she let him. His fingers ran over the bones at the back of her hand and she opened her fingers to let his slide between them, then both hands curled together into loose nestled fists. 'Everyone's backing me at the station,' he said, 'but I know what they're all thinking.'

'You did nothing wrong, Dan.'

'It doesn't feel that way.'

'But it's true.'

'I never killed anyone before.'

'He'd have killed you if he could.'

She rose from her place at the end of the bed, peeled off her gown and began to dress slowly. Her clothes lay neatly folded on the seat of her dressing table's padded chair, her bra draped over the chair's back. To feel better about himself, Dan turned away, allowing her a little privacy, then wearily he got up and began to dress, too.

There wasn't much more to say. He wished that he could have seen Quillan, just to tie together in his mind exactly how the whole thing had happened. As it was, the vagueness left too much room for second-guessing. He had no recollection at all of how close to the top of the stairs they had been during the struggle, but it must have been close or Quillan couldn't possibly have fallen. Dan had his injuries, actual physical evidence, to back his story; one of the uniformed men – Kelly, he seemed to think – found him slumped on the landing floor, barely conscious from the pain and with blood seeping from his eyes, and then the medical reports confirmed the gouging. This fact alone should be enough to put him in the clear with the enquiry board. But if something more was required then he could surely count on his reputation of some thirty-four years of almost unsullied lawful service to stack up well against the dirty past of a drug dealer and long-term addict who had nothing much to his name but a string of convictions and a history of violence. The enquiry would find a way to overlook the few black marks that lingered around his name. When it came to things like this, police looked after their own.

Before he left the bedroom, he slipped his wallet from his trousers pocket and drew out four fifties. Anna made a show of studying herself in the dressing table's vanity mirror and then tying up her hair with a piece of elastic so that she wouldn't have to see him fold the notes once and then again. He tucked the money under the bedside alarm clock, just as always. Sometimes he left less, sometimes more, depending on the current state of his finances. They never talked about it, because it would be embarrassing and because the pretence allowed them both to imagine their situation to be something more than the reality. He always remembered her birthday, and Christmas, though two or three months could often pass without them seeing one another.

He had twenty years on her, he told himself, and he was out of shape, a stubborn old fool, stuck in his ways. Nothing that she needed. Still, he hoped that she wasn't like this with the others.

In the hallway, she kissed him, almost shyly. 'Let me know what happens on Tuesday,' she said. 'I'll be waiting to hear.'

He nodded that he would.

These were always the worst moments for him. Leaving her, and knowing that he was about to face back into the emptiness of his life again. In the pause that followed, he almost told her that he loved her, but of course he didn't. She probably knew anyway. Her fingers held gently to the crook of his elbow, keeping the connection for as long as possible.

The real question, of course, was not the issue of self-defence but that of reasonable force. Wiley and the others at the station knew better than to say it, but they were all thinking it. The first knee to the groin was justified, maybe even the second, but where did reasonable end and excessive begin? He wished that he could remember the whole thing more clearly. Had he stopped after the pressure on his eyes had loosened and fallen away, or had he recognised a chance? And it was natural to push the lumbering weight away, or it would have been, if the stairs wasn't so close.

As gently as he could, he pulled from Anna's touch and stepped outside. Night had taken hold and a cold easterly wind was blowing, the gusts loosely clotted with flecks of rain. 'Take care, Anna,' he said, but he held his gaze fixed to the darkness. Then he broke away from the shelter of the doorway and ran the few yards to his car. He waited until the light flared up behind her curtained window before starting the engine. He hated goodbyes.

REMEMBERING BRIAN

It must have been a fortnight at least before the tears and the tantrums stopped and we had all settled down and accepted that we were here for the long term. School. There were eleven of us in the class, and for that first fortnight we took our turns at trying to escape, at pleading with our mothers that if they only took us home we swear we wouldn't be an ounce of trouble. If even one of us could have made it then it meant that there'd be hope for us all, but two weeks in and it became clear that nobody was listening. We were junior infants now, and that was it.

Brian Culley was almost six. His late start was due to a bout of polio which had left him with a curvature of the spine. He could walk now, but badly; he had to wear iron frames the length of his legs. Caterpillars, he called them, when we gathered round during our lunch break in the small yard behind the school, mixing up the actual word, callipers, with the crawling yellow insects that we liked to collect because they made girls cry if used in certain unexpected ways. He showed us how the bars were held in place, and told us what his mother had told him, that if he didn't wear them he'd be a hunchback by the time he made his Holy Communion. We all thought that would look great in the photographs, but we didn't say it because we didn't really know Brian yet. Even with his stoop, he was the tallest in the class by a good six inches, and because of his bout of illness had been fed to excess, so he was easily the heaviest of us too. And just because he couldn't walk right didn't mean that he couldn't fight.

A fortnight in and the days were already being lost in a stupor. Miss Moynihan, our teacher, was a slight, shrill woman, pushing fifty and going nowhere. She dyed her hair a shade of brown that looked far too rich to be real, and she wore it in a bouffant style that didn't suit her sharp, angular features at all. It was Brian who christened her with the fitting nickname of Bull's Eye, and we all snickered at that and whispered it among ourselves. Her eyes were the immediate point of focus on her face, great dark hyper-thyroid bulges that fixed on you while her constantly quivering mouth churned out chill ribbons of criticism. 'I'm so disappointed in you, Billy,' she'd say, and we were supposed to hang our heads at that and act contrite, act disappointed in ourselves. Brian though, would just stare back, and sometimes, just for fun, he'd turn his own eyes ever so slightly. Miss Moynihan wouldn't know what to do with him then, so she'd make him go and sit in the corner. The rest of us she made stand, but Brian's mother insisted that because of the leg braces, standing wasn't recommended for long periods. It could cause him irreparable damage, apparently.

'Take your seat and move to the corner, Brian,' Miss Moynihan would squeal, and Brian would sigh and make a drama of rising and dragging his chair across the floor, purposely crashing into desk after desk just to make us laugh. The corner was no hardship to him; actually, it was a break from lessons.

I quickly discovered that there was a stifling tedium to

school. Apart from the fifteen minutes or so of fun that we'd have at playtime, the day was spent just sitting, copying down the first few letters of the alphabet from the blackboard into our workbooks. Or learning our tables. One and one is two; two and one is three; on and on. Two weeks to a four-year-old on the cusp of five feels like an eternity. Everyone felt the same, but we had Brian.

Because he was older than us he was better at almost everything. He could already write his name, and he could count to sixty in English and twenty in Irish. Because of this, school must have been even more boring to him, and he used every opportunity to cause a disruption. Miss Moynihan was uncertain how best to deal with him. We were far easier to punish; she could slap us or make us stand outside the door. But she quickly learned that it wasn't wise to slap Brian. The one time she tried it, just a mild crack across the hands with her own, his face crumpled so completely and the sobs were so wrenching that he actually caused her to flee the classroom. We had been sure that he was just pretending, the sight of him wailing, his eyes clenched shut and the slits almost lost in the heavy folds of his face, his mouth stretched wide and his tongue lolling free on bleating waves. But after the teacher had left the room he kept on, a full ten minutes until finally she returned and pressed some sweets into his hand and told him to take them into the corner and to please be quiet. Even then, he quieted only gradually, and while we worked at our sums we could hear him sucking noisily on a Peggy's Leg and still occasionally shuddering with tears. Miss Moynihan never hit him again, though she kept on hitting us even when we tried to react as he had done.

The day I remember best stretches back to that time.

Brian had the desk next to me. All day long he'd draw covert stick pictures of the teacher or of other people in the village, like Fr Lucey, the parish priest, or Joan Kelly's grandmother who had a great strawberry birthmark smeared across her face. I'd never know who he was drawing; my job was to guess.

'That's oul' Bull's Eye, boy. Sittin' on the ponny.' Nobody used the ponny any more; a lot was changing in the country, and backyard toilets were just about a thing of the past, but there was something about the word, especially when put in conjunction with teachers, something so undignified, that it was an essential feature of any of Brian's matchstick masterworks.

I'd study the picture again armed with this new information, and if the teacher happened to be writing on the blackboard I'd risk a snicker behind a shielding hand.

Brian was the only child in the class with a schoolbag, a small brown patent leather satchel that rarely held more than a jam sandwich, a pencil, and his workbook. The rest of us carried our workbook under our arms. Our pencils we tucked up on our ears, the way some of our fathers did with their cigarettes if they were down to their last one. We admired Brian's schoolbag, and we knew that he was proud of it.

This particular morning, when he raised the bag from the floor and flashed a quick grin in my direction, I simply thought that he was about to unveil his latest masterpiece, a scribble of Miss Moynihan hanging by the neck from a tree, or something equally tasteful. But the bag this morning carried a more notable weight.

It was mid September, but summer still had a strong hold. A blaze of yellow sunlight streamed through the windows and lit the classroom more brightly than ever before. It was warm too, even Miss Moynihan was wearing only a long dark skirt and a high-necked apple-green blouse instead of her usual layers of cardigans and woollen sweaters.

'Hey, Bill,' Brian hissed, loud enough, I was sure, for everyone in the room to hear. 'Guess what I have in the bag.'

I shrugged my shoulders. 'I don't know,' I said. 'A picture?'

His smile was wide and there was a wicked set to his clenched teeth. 'Not even close, boy.'

I watched his small fat hands fumble with the leather strap and brass buckle. The knuckles were little puncture holes in the flesh. Soon, everyone was watching, everyone except the teacher. He shared the wicked grin around, then pushed a hand inside the bag, held it there for a moment so as to heighten the suspense, and withdrew a huge dead rat.

Somebody screamed, and then everybody did. It was like an offer of freedom, and we screamed for all we were worth. All of us, even Brian. Brian tossed the dead rat into the air and it bounced off a desk closer to the front before its weight brought it to the floor. Miss Moynihan turned from the blackboard and looked terrified without quite knowing why. Then she saw the rat and scrambled up onto a chair. Her weight set the chair to tottering and after a moment when I was sure it would find its balance it went over, spilling her badly. The rat had landed as though crouched and readying itself to attack. Miss Moynihan lay on the floor some three or four feet from it, and she screamed, her bulging eyes huge in her pale face.

Brian sprung from his place, grabbed the rat by the tail and began to swing it over his head. Somewhere behind him, the door was thrown open as the other teachers hurried to see what all the commotion was about. When they saw Brian spinning the rat they stopped short. We watched as he swung and swung, the rat a blur of grey fur above his head. Then, suddenly, the tail broke off and the body of the rat smashed into the wall with a sickening crunch. It slipped a bloody trail to the floor and lay in a mangled heap at the skirting board.

None of the teachers knew that Brian had brought the rat to school; they all assumed that he had simply picked it up and killed it. He was the last of us to work that out, but he did in the space of a few seconds. 'It was a rat,' he said needlessly, the words squeezing out between great wet heaves of breath. 'I just saw it there and I killed it.'

Mr Hennessy, the teacher of the class next door, moved across the room, stooped to study the dead rat, then rose and helped Miss Moynihan to her feet. She was crying, gagging on her own tears. 'Now take it easy, Loretta,' he said, in a voice that didn't know how to get below strict. 'It's all right. Young Brian there saved the day ...'

For a while, Brian and I were friends. More than that, even; we were inseparable. He was so mischievous, and I couldn't help but look up to him. But as the years passed and we moved up through the ranks of school, different paths led us in different directions. Drifting apart didn't happen overnight, but was a gradual thing. New friends came and old ones went. By Confirmation age, we were little more than nodding acquaintances, running in different circles, our lives full of different priorities.

Sometimes, though, we will cross paths in one or another of the village pubs. The age gap that was so alluring then means nothing at all now; middle age loses all such subtleties. And when we do meet, we put our respective lives on hold for half an hour or so and share our memories over a pint, laughing at things that weren't all that funny at the time but which have lost their pain thanks to the passing of years. We'll chat and laugh, calling to mind stories and faces long since past, and on the best nights a glimmer of our childhood friendship will spark to life again.

WAR SONG

Thirty-five years, and even now, some things feel as close as yesterday. For instance, all it takes to relive the day that I probably should have died is for me to close my eyes and let it in again. Clenching them shut, because the darkness beyond is the link, bringing me back to the place where bad things lurk.

That day, that ugly early morning, eyes clenched against the war, and all the world is darkness. There is pain, but mostly there is the fear. An all-pervasive thing, and smothering. The mud slick against my face, the spears of rain pummelling. Noise made up of differing levels: the faraway rumble of thunder or falling mortars; the whine and fizz of bullets and sometimes their dull thud as they find their target; the jerk of a shocked breath torn free. And then, after a wet flapping draw of air, the screams. My own screams too, thin and distant sounding but mine because they taste like mine. Voices of others, like Pete Sanchez calling for a medic, Jimmy Testeverde crying Jesus in blood bubbles over and over, his mouth torn to shreds. Above, Dave Gelman telling me to just take it easy, to lie back for the sake of all that's good and holy, it's over, going home time.

And the bullet, big as the world and hot as hell somewhere in my stomach. Gelman's Texan drawl: Got yourself a ticket wound, Scruggs. A Purple Heart and a magic ticket home. Thank the Lord for this sweet gook bullet, kid. Out of here, and don't you be coming back now. Got that?

The mud has the taste of foreign places. The way the roasted air of Egypt tastes of spice, the grey mud of Vietnam clots every inch of exposed flesh and is drawn deep by the tongue's nervous, darting stroke and swallowed, coating the mouth and throat like rotting olive oil, tasting of sourness and steel, the nutrients of the soil or all the poisons that have been dropped with the intention only to kill, to do anything that has to be done to win, at any cost. It is a taste that exists in smell and even in touch, a thing to batter senses, heightened and desperate enough to smother even the contesting stench of my own burning flesh.

I try to sit up, just suddenly to see that I still can, but Davie Gelman is there, and pushing me back down again and again, that big hand hard against my shoulder, that black face shining like an eclipse against the day. 'JUST CHILL, SCRUGGS!' Roaring to be heard as a dust-off drowns out the world, all the words and the lash and lash of the rain percussive in the mangroves and the buzz and distant crack of enemy fire arriving and volleyed back, the speed of sound perverting everything, bullets past before singing out their take-off. I try to sit up because I am afraid. It feels as though I have just one leg.

Then I am down again, back down in the mud, made so this time not by an endless push but by Gelman's big right hand shaping a fist and then driven hard into my face. Now along with the mud I can taste the warm and sickly seep of my own blood sluicing through my teeth, filling the pocket of my sinus. But still what I mostly taste is the mud.

'HAD TO DO IT, SCRUGGS!' Gelman is saying,

beneath the shuffle of the rotors. Shuffling like the MG's, the guys back in Rear Echelon like to say, grasping for the coolness to cloak their feeling of inadequacy. Wonder when Booker T's gonna get here? And to the helicopter pilots: What did you guys have for lunch, huh? Green Onions? And that bastard Gelman thinks HAD TO DO IT, SCRUGGS is going to be good enough! When I get up I'll kick that bastard's black ass a new hole, don't give a shit how big he thinks he is.

Spearing me in the good leg then, and looking down I can see the syrette in my thigh like a child's dart, jogging with the twitch of muscle gone spastic, but I can't see the morphine or even feel it. I have seen guys getting pinned with those little syrette things before and often wondered what it would be like to get the morphine myself, and now finally my turn comes and that bastard Gelman sticks me with a dud. Just wait till I can get up to that low-down son of a bitch. Medic, my ass! When I get a hold of him he'll wish to God his mammy never met his daddy. Bastard!

The rotors slow in a way that I have never heard before, and for a moment I am actually afraid for them, afraid that they have been taken down by enemy fire and are about to blow, but then voices of the men begin to catch the strangeness too, words elongate with the same demented frustration as running underwater and the day's colours seem to dim, and I think, this is it, this is the morphine, and I might have been wrong about Gelman after all, because Gelman's a hell of a good guy really and that's the God's honest truth.

There is the idea too, just some faraway logic, that maybe this is the other it, the dying it. Maybe this is what it's like when you're dying, your eyes playing tricks and the stinking taste of mud in your throat.

I hold with that idea though only until I feel that bastard Gelman's hand inside my stomach, his big thin fingers searching for the bullet probably, because that's all that can be in there since even my corned beef hash lunch had decided to pull out for the safety of the foxhole floor, and I try to tell myself that I'm not that close to the end, not yet anyway, can't be. I'm not ready yet to die. All of this is just a mistake.

This must be as bad as it ever gets. I can feel the spreading coldness and I know that I have been ripped apart. Without having to look, without having to relive the moment of impact in my mind. I know it, and I know it is bad. So standing on the brink, what else is there that is left to fear? Nothing surely, because the worst has already happened.

Well, there is death, but pain is the opposite of death, right? And surely all of this hurts too much. But maybe we've all got it wrong; it might be that death is a thing of endless suffering, an eternity of tasting mud and the ceaseless rain beating you into the ground and taking your watered-down blood in rivulets down into the earth to make sure that even when you leave this place you can never really leave as long as a part of you remains.

Just thank sweet Jesus that Gelman's fingers are thin.

I hope you washed your hands, Davie, I want to say, just as a joke, but my mouth and throat are busy screaming and there is no room for words. I am not really screaming because of the pain – though it seems to be driving free from every pore – but because shot men scream, and men with other men's fingers in their stomachs do nothing else but scream and scream until they die.

After that is mostly in and out, nothing real, nothing imagined, the drugs perhaps or maybe me just veering close to the death I no longer suddenly fear quite so much. I can feel it coming sometimes like the tide, the wash of the ocean approaching and rolling back, approaching and rolling back, but approaching an indecipherable step closer every time and rolling back just a little less. And then it is so close that it floods over my face, smothering. Death tastes just like mud. When it ebbs again I gasp for air, choking because the air is water too, water and mud.

I am moving and what else is there to do but look up as men take me by the arms and legs. Ebbons at my right arm, glancing down at me from time to time and smiling and saying something that I don't hear but something that I just know must be funny because Ebbons is the funniest guy you'll ever meet and because if it makes that fucking madman smile then it must be funny. Quincy has my left arm, though he doesn't look down at me at all because, can you believe this, even after five months In Country, the son of a bitch is squeamish. Can't stand the sight of blood. If Quincy's not looking down at me, then it's a safe bet that I'm bleeding pretty bad. And, you know, in a way maybe that's not such a terrible thing, because knowing I am bleeding makes me realise, on some level anyway, that this game can still go either way, and that if I really want to get through this then I'll have to pull damn hard.

Except, I can't pull any more. Suddenly, I am so tired. All the months of marching, all the nights too wired to sleep, are dragging now at my bones. Sleep is calling me, and nothing else seems to matter very much.

Faces lose their identity and become shadows, pale in the light and heavier when the light wanes, and the numb, featureless sky is a falling whiteness, wanting ground only. The men carry me along, and I can feel my body drooping between them like the hang of a hammock, can feel myself swaying softly as they wade and stumble through the milky water and over the muddy ridges of the paddy field.

Against the pleading call of sleep, the pain seems less, and I know that this must be the morphine, and above the silhouettes of my comrades the sky is nothing but that falling whiteness, full of the spears of rain. And then through the slosh and suck of fallen steps there is the whiplash echo of the rotors, the perfect 2/4 time tucka-TUCKA tucka-TUCKA rhythm of the blades, and when their edges stray into the whiteness, they are like a band-saw, a shadowy arc made hypnotic with illusive speed.

On the chopper's bed I lie back and listen to the other wounded men. Where has this calmness come from? Sleep is a gloom, everywhere now, threatening with the siren's call. Go on, I tell myself. What difference can it make if it is now or in an hour? I close my eyes and listen to the music.

Can it still be only morning, that morning I should have died? Where am I now? Saigon? At some China Beach Med Evac? Stateside? Any one of these seems vaguely possible, but surely I am not still banked along the Cam Lo River. Surely I am not still spread out in this fifty-acre cage of paddy, that rippled black corrugate ground, with its hollows sumptuous in stagnant rainwater, that empty plain punctured with the slashmarks of the plough.

Off in the background, the rotors keep their perfect tucka-TUCKA 2/4 rhythm and the cries of the other fallen men rise to meet them in a kind of Gregorian chant, and I know that if I open my eyes I will see those sounds swirl and spiral, and it will be the morphine for certain because isn't that what morphine makes you see? But in the dark innards of the helicopter I just listen to the troubled jazz of the screams, weaving and sighing on the harsh breath and bass moans, a troubled chorus tardy against the wasting dawn.

A voice punctures the terrible morning lilt, 'ALL RIGHT, DANNY. THAT'S THE LOT!' and an engine roars like something wild, and then we are climbing and I have to swim back to the surface to keep from rolling.

A body jolts free of its stretcher and collides with me, and I open my eyes and see a creature contorted against his own end, the exposed bones of the ruined face a glaring yellow sunshine against the darkness. A smiling face, all perfect teeth exposed by the mortar fallout that I have seen before, the flesh and gum that used to be a mouth and lips hanging in ropes from the jutting chin. There are sounds, bubbling from his throat, but no mouth means shapeless words, bad sounds only. One eye stares at me, pleading for something that I don't want to consider, and there is nothing to do but look away and try to think of any other thing but this and my own possible end as we, the damned few, tilt and roll and sail still skyward.

Gelman is right; the fighting for me is done, and all that is left now is to live or to die. The morphine is a pretence as the pain of my wounds begins to rise again.

THE HUNCHBACK

The sweet things were what kept him coming back, Marguerite's casual way of leaving half a slab of chocolate on the yard table after it had grown too dark to paint outside. She liked to paint in the evening time, those couple of dusky summer hours after the day was done but with the night still holding back, and August was a perfect month for it, the mildest part of the season before the Atlantic brought its fall-time chill. From her back garden the land fell away, affording her a perfect view of the cove, the village with its small old multicoloured homes shaping a neat boomerang around the ceaseless press of the sea. She'd set up her easel after eating a light supper and paint until the light was all but lost, impressionistic oil-on-canvas studies of this island world that she was still, even after four years, striving to understand. Four years of trying to depict the many subtle shades of a domineering three-quarter length sky and the constant, irresistible ebb and roll of an ever-changing sea, and then sifting through the resultant chaff in search of the few that she deemed worthy of survival.

The first time she noticed him he was stooped among the briars of a hawthorn bush, and when she called out, startled, he panicked and ran. For a hunchback he moved with deft speed; his low bobbing head and the swaying cant of his shoulders looked clumsy, but he had an immaculate sense of balance, a skill surely perfected out of necessity. The evening she had first seen him, she watched as he tore from the hawthorn and charged headlong down the incline, and though her heart was beating a hard pulse up into her throat, being gifted those seconds to study him as he fled allowed her to consider and dismiss her initial fears. His right arm flailed as he ran, stirring the air and keeping him upright, and his body rocked from side to side, the great hump on his back obscuring his low-hung head.

When he slipped behind the flash of granite that poked upward from the tufted yellow grass some hundred yards or so below Marguerite's garden, she knew she had him trapped, and she could picture him down there, crouched down and pressed into the hollow of the hillside, swallowing deep whoops of the cool evening air and probably shaking with the shock and adrenaline of having been discovered. Briefly she considered making her way down after him, just to tell him that it was all right for him to come and watch her paint, that he needn't have run and that she was sorry for calling out, really she was. But while her fear felt tempered by the pity in her heart, it didn't dissipate completely. She stood there in her garden, her arms folded across her narrow chest, and watched until it grew late enough for the shadows to merge and the hillside to grow indistinct, and finally she went inside, telling herself that he'd probably have made use of the darkness to get away and that her journey down would have been a wasted one.

'Lucky you', her friends always said, after the small talk had run its course. They weren't really friends, not in any connected way, because Marguerite wasn't the sort of person who cultivated genuine relationships, not any more. They were acquaintances, people she met through her painting, gallery owners or collectors mostly, wealthy women with too much time on their hands and bound by a certain lifestyle to rich, uninterested men. They tolerated her, she supposed, because she provided them with quality work, and also because she was far away. A few minutes of talking on the telephone every couple of months or so, and possibly an afternoon's lunch in one of the better restaurants during one of her very occasional sojourns to London, or Dublin, was a price that they were willing to pay. She knew that they liked to be able to drop her name at really important parties and to speak about her in that intimate way of close friendships, and maybe they did see a certain amount of romance in the way she had chosen to live, even though they wouldn't have swapped lives with her for the world. 'Lucky old you,' they always said, when ten minutes or so had passed, time filled to overflowing with the usual inane banter. 'Throwing off the shackles, living in an island paradise.'

'It's only West Cork,' she'd laugh, playing her part in the game, giving what was expected of her. 'But it can be paradise when the sun is shining and the breeze is blowing just right.' It wouldn't have done to make mention of what was really in her heart, the truth that, far from being a romantic and carefree existence, the loneliness could at times be suffocating. Occasionally, one of them would ask, with all the crudity of their sort of friendship: 'And what do you do for manly company, sweetheart?' Unashamedly prying, with more than a hint of mockery in their tone. She had over the years developed a way of fielding such a question though, and she'd laugh it off, because that was a better response than examining the truth of her situation. Or if her mood was such, she often replied with something like, 'You do realise that there are other people on this island, don't you, dear? I mean, it's hardly Robinson Crusoe, is it?' Almost smelling the two or three glasses of afternoon Chardonnay through the telephone's receiver, conscious of how the good wine tainted and slurred the interrogator's breath, she'd try hard to keep from screaming.

Later, after her state of silence had been resumed, she'd think about the conversation, examine the various nuances of things discussed and inferred, and sometimes her loneliness grew to crushing proportions and she'd slump down in her favourite armchair and give in to the aching push of tears.

There were available men in the village, certain rugged middle-aged types, the only ones left who were not married or who had not run off in search of better, easier lives on the mainland. Men who still drew their livelihood from the sea, wrestling with nets and foraging among the waves in search of the ever-diminishing shoals of herring. Or, increasingly, men who had given up the fishing life to run pleasure cruises and harbour tours, who organised deep-water angling expeditions that were actually only pantomimes of reality, for the amusement and entertainment of tourists with more money than sense. Marguerite often saw these men in the village, their rough clothes clinging desperately to their bulk, their windblown faces set with that familiar braced expression, and she had enough of an imagination to consider how their flesh would feel, how the smell of salt water would radiate from them, and how their rough hands would caress her, the rasp of their scarred skin in no way gentle but still, for all of that, companionable, and maybe compassionate. It was irresistible to fall for the stereotypical thoughts of a crudeness borne by the only way of life they had ever known, and it didn't matter much that she knew they couldn't be that simple, that they had to be much more than masses of hardship-bulk, that they needed to think and feel about the world just like the most sophisticated city dweller. Much better though, she had quickly decided, to ignore that sort of understanding, because it tended to complicate the fantasy. Just like knowing how a magic trick is really done, or the threadbare, uninspiring truth behind a favourite song.

The telephone conversations always ended the same way, the usual fluttered excuse from the other end of the line, a fair-weather friend consumed by the hectic excesses of a city lifestyle. 'Well, it's been lovely to chat with you, Margie, but I really must be getting along. I have an appointment for highlights at three, and there is still a world of things to do before I'm ready. We can't all have it as good as you, I'm afraid.' The gurgle of laughter that followed then was always a lie, and they both knew it, because that type of person had given up the free life in exchange for a big house, some well-addressed eight- or ten-bedroom spread with two or even more expensive new cars outside in the tree-lined driveway, a ridiculously generous monthly allowance, and a husband who, for all his lack of interest, still came home every night and still needed and provided the gestures of love. Such friends liked to say often that Marguerite had everything, the freedom to do and say whatever she wished and to go wherever the humour took her, but a minute after they had hung up the phone all thoughts of Marguerite and her island ways were forgotten until a month or two from now when her name would come up at some party to remind them that another call might be in order, or when they came into a windfall of money that needed flaunting and a new painting seemed like the ideal way to go about it. To them, freedom was one of those ideas that seemed better in theory than in practice, and in the end it was a simple matter of priorities.

Gradually, the giddy pleasures of their voices faded from Marguerite's mind and the stillness of her small rundown living-room took hold, and she'd look around her, searching among the clutter of books, bric-à-brac and unframed, half-finished paintings for some small element of joy that would help her bear the stomach-blow of loneliness. Her old albums leaned against the wall beneath the window, and she played them constantly, not too loud, just enough to dispel the silence. Mid-1960s rock, some Outlaw country, and a smattering of folk; meaningful words offered in rich or weary voices, preaching truths even as they painted pictures. She treated the records well, carefully replacing them in their sleeves, or blowing dust from their surface and breathing their dark vinyl smell before laying them gently on the turntable. She knew all the words to the Creedence songs and usually sang along, though with the Beatles or Dylan she was more selective with her singing, not wanting to get in the way of what those songs had to say. As though there was some danger that she might actually have missed their message.

At first, the idea that someone was watching her felt a little frightening. She was thirty-seven years old, and while her looks had given up the refined honing demanded while living in a city, what pushed through, after such trifling things as make-up and skin care products had been abandoned, was a sort of earthy beauty. She could look at her reflection in the mirror now upon rising and no longer cringe but actually take pride in the first creep of crow's feet spreading from the corner of her eyes or the hairline slivers that meshed the skin around her shrinking mouth. This reflection felt like the real her, the person she was without the mask that she had worn for so many years, a mask always endured for the benefit of others. Well, men hadn't fallen for the mask, never for any significant length of time, anyway, and there was relief in being able to abandon such a façade. It felt like the island's welcoming gift to her.

Here on the island there was no need to try impressing anyone; she could be the person she really was. And it felt as though a great weight had been lifted from her shoulders. In the village, walking down by the pier, she pretended not to notice how the men looked at her as they worked snags from their fishing nets, and they never bothered her though she knew that they probably talked behind her back. She was still a stranger, after all. And she only went down by the water when she was feeling good, not trusting herself when the loneliness reached desperate proportions. When that loneliness closed in she stayed at home and listened to her records or, if the evening was fine, set up her easel in the back garden and painted whatever type of sky lay spread out to the west. Trying to work away her sense of disillusion.

An art critic had once written a well-received thesis for one of the more established art journals on her ability to infiltrate every human emotion into the singular setting of a skyscape, and though she wasn't always aware that she was even doing it, reading those words did ring true with her. The sky changed so much over the island that she had reached a point now where she never needed to paint anything else. Bloodstained sunsets, pale summer dawns, the ochre looming of a building thunder storm; the muddy slop of her oils on canvas channelled all her pleasures and her pains, and the gaping sky played psychiatric Rorschach games, always searching for some better understanding of her own internal world.

She was shocked to find the hunchback watching her from the hawthorn.

A few nights after the first encounter she caught sight of him again, detecting just a slight unnatural stirring in the hawthorn bushes. This time, she used all her willpower to ignore it, and when the evening had grown too dark to paint she packed her things and went inside, purposely leaving the half slab of chocolate on the table, along with an untouched pint of milk. And once inside it was she who became the voyeur, crouching low beside the kitchen window and watching for her admirer's approach. He made her wait until it was completely dark, the better part of an hour according to the slow pulse of the wall-clock, and her hamstrings ached and began to cramp from stooping there so long, her balance kept by her narrow shoulder set against the wall and the tips of her fingers pressing a steel grip on the whitewashed sill. Her heart pounded with every uncertain stirring or sound, and a dozen times or more she was almost on the point of giving up, telling herself that this was ridiculous, that surely he was gone by now because no one would stand in the middle of a hawthorn bush for this long in the darkness. There'd be spiders, maybe even rats. But another voice in her head persuaded her otherwise, insisting that she could afford five more minutes now that she had waited this long, and really, what else had she to do apart from sitting in her living-room or lying in bed struggling to get interested in some trashy novel. If waiting here by the window could set her heart to beating this way, then was that really so bad? Surely she could put up with the hardship of a few aches in exchange for a flush of excitement that made her feel so alive.

When he did finally move, she almost missed it. By then the night had grown so dark, coming on for midnight and with what little sliver of moon there was limited to timid flashes through the cloaking oaks that skirted the southern boundary of her garden, she felt certain that it was simply her mind playing more of its tricks. But by the time he reached the garden table her eyes had adjusted to his shape, and she found better focus still when the cracked moon crept into view, its glow spotlighting him enough for her to see how he had to further contort his body's posture in order to drink the milk, how raising the bottle to his mouth forced his hump leftwards and down in a way that made her gasp with a sense of pity. Through the thin glass she could hear his laboured efforts as the milk wrestled against his breath, and though the details were hidden she felt that in the asthmatic efforts of that sound, she had come to know him. The last of the fear in her heart gave way and became something else, something close to understanding.

The darkness gave him courage, and when he had finished the milk he lay the empty bottle carefully down on the table, put the piece of chocolate in his shirt pocket, and set about exploring the garden. Cautiously, but as someone comfortable with the techniques of stealth. There were no lights burning in the house and hadn't been for the better part of an hour; Marguerite hoped to give the impression that she had gone to bed. From the lowest corner of the window she watched him move away from the table and across the yard. The moon cast its glow from behind, making a blackness of his face, and she couldn't tell if the lurching movement was simply a feature of his natural walk or if he was repeatedly stealing glances at the upstairs windows, frightened that he was being observed. He had such an ungainly walk, and yet she couldn't ignore its rare and obvious fluency, a rhythm to his swaying almost musical in its tempo.

When she realised that he had veered his wandering and was now moving directly towards the window, she dropped abruptly to her knees and pressed herself hard against the wall. Her pulse raced and she was convinced that he had seen her, that her movement had been too sudden and that even in the darkness it must have caught his eye. Within seconds she could feel him above her, leaning against the glass, cupping his hands together as a shield against the moon's glare and peering inside. The glass squeaked in its old frame, but held. Sweat streamed from her dishevelled hairline, caressing her temples and then her cheeks. She held her breath; the night had grown unaccountably cool.

Eventually he tired of looking at nothing much and moved away. She could feel him go, and she knew it from how the moonlight poured across the linoleum floor of the kitchen, refreshed after its eclipse, but even though it was safe now to move she continued to hold her position, as though she owed something to this hiding place. Finally though, she did raise herself to risk looking outside, but by then a long time had passed, and the garden was empty.

'That's only Tadhg Maloney.' Bennie Cuthbert looked up from the bucket scales full of potatoes, a 2lb weight nothing at all in his big open hand. 'Has he been up along to you, then?'

Marguerite stood, trying to decide between two cans of Campbell's soup: Country Vegetable or Scotch Broth. She shrugged her shoulders. 'No, nothing like that. I was out walking over along the Carrick cliffs that fine day we had last week. Sunday, I think it was. And I saw him. I was just curious, that's all.' She hoped that the casual strain in her voice sounded believable, and rather than have to face the shopkeeper's studying glare she busied herself with reading the ingredients on the label of the Scotch Broth.

'Well, them that know him say he's a harmless sort. I don't have much business with him myself, though I knew his people well enough and I have to say that they were all decent stock. Except for an uncle he had who took a queer turn and was taken off to the red brick in Cork city.'

'The red brick?'

In explanation Bennie smirked, then rolled his eyes and tapped his temple with a stubby index finger. 'Took to shooting at fishing boats from Ban Head, he did. The men all knew enough to stay well out, but the rocks saw to that anyway. It can be treacherous around there if the wind's blowing. A boat would come a cropper in a hurry if it drifted in too close to shore around that part of the island. Anyway, there was no danger of him actually hitting anyone, but did that stop him? Not one bit of it. He'd stand up there, ould Seamus would, and he'd blaze away with his double-barrel, raining buckshot down into the sea. The men would stand up in their boats and watch him. A few used to cheer when the pellets would fall short but most of them just muttered a few prayers and let the currents take them past. Ould Seamus was a bit gone in the head by then, used to say he was battling the invaders, but there was a time when he could clear a field of hay all by himself, and he was mighty when it came to cutting turf, had a set of shoulders on him like a Holstein bull.'

Marguerite drifted around the small shop, gathering items from the shelves and dropping them in her basket. Supplies that would see her through another week, things like dried pasta, jars of tomato sauce, cheese. 'Where does he live?' she asked, when she made it finally to the counter.

'Who, Tadhg? Oh, they have a place over on the southern side of the island, just himself and his mother. Hannah. She doesn't leave the house any more. The last priest we had here used to visit her once a week, for a chat I suppose and to give her Communion, but then he was moved to a parish in Kerry. Father Hassett replaced him, and he's an all right sort, from Inchigeela, but he got a feed of abuse whenever he tried to call and after a while he just gave up on her. They say she's like one of them women you see on the television from America, the ones who keep eating until they're too big to even stand up. Some of the people from over that side of the island have it that she must be up around the thirty stone mark now. Course, there could be a bit of exaggeration in that, but still, it's true enough that she's never seen outside any more, not even on the hottest days. Tadhg runs the errands, what little they need doing. Their ould cottage is falling down around them, broken windows, sunken thatch, the place is red rotten. They have a couple of acres, a decent enough piece of ground, and Big Tom, a bed in heaven to him, that'd be Tadhg's father, used to get the best out of it until he dropped down dead one night while turning a drill of potatoes. That ground is gone to ruin now, all overgrown and thick with rocks, good for little beyond breeding rats.'

She watched Bennie study the price tag on each item,

the values handwritten in blue ink and barely legible, before calculating the final tally on the old-fashioned register. He didn't look too bad for a man on the generous side of fifty. There was no wedding ring in evidence, but there was a wife, Maura, a dowdy creature with small eyes and a thick, unhappy face. Marguerite held out the money, thinking how funny it was that there seemed to be someone for everyone but that a person only really noticed when they themselves were all alone.

Bennie meticulously calculated her change, and she nodded her thanks when he handed her some coins, not bothering to check whether or not the returned sum was correct.

'Tadhg is harmless,' he repeated, just as she reached the shop door. 'But if he's bothering you at all, it might be worth mentioning to Sergeant Twomey. The sergeant has a good way with a quiet word, and that'll be an end to it.'

Her smile was meant to show gratitude for his concern, but it felt brittle to her and probably looked it, too. 'No,' she said. 'I'm fine, really. I was just curious, that's all. You know how it is.'

The summer pushed on, colours softened, and the visits of Tadhg became more frequent, until there were evenings when Marguerite would catch herself actually waiting for his arrival. In the depths of her loneliness, she found something flattering in the idea that anyone cared and admired her enough to come and watch as she toiled with her latest slathered depiction of a sunset sky. Even though he was a hunchback, a tortured, outcast soul who wrestled constantly with isolation and despair, she had grown to rely on his presence. When she painted, the headland rocks became the rounded bulge of his hump, and the moiling sea and sweeping winds whispered his innermost secrets.

She no longer felt even a hint of fear any more either. The passing weeks had helped her grow accustomed to the idea of him as a feature in her life.

While on her way down to the village one afternoon to stock up on some provisions, she passed him on the narrow road. On impulse, she smiled and said hello. He flinched, stepped into the grassy dyke on his side of the road and almost stumbled. Then he hurried on his way, not making any attempt at a reply, though she could feel the intensity in his eyes as he studied her. Memorising the details, perhaps.

He wasn't bad looking. There was something not quite right about his face, the muscles set in a certain way as though used to bearing pain, but his features were finely balanced, and he had the most striking eyes she had ever seen. A vague blue the shade of cigarette smoke in a particular sort of light. Pale and only half-aware. If she hadn't known he was just thirty years old she would have put him down as late forties, but that sense of premature aging was nothing unusual for the men on this island, men with flesh used to the worst elements of a bolstering sea wind, their hides thickened by suffering. Perhaps it was the island that made the hump on his back far less repulsive to her than it would have seemed had their paths crossed in Dublin or in London; maybe it was some overdeveloped level of compassion on her part, one made so insistent by her exile.

When she lived in London she had seemed so refined. Not a snob, never that, but she mixed with a particular sort of crowd and rarely drifted beyond that sphere. There were demands, and expectations. The eccentric element of her nature came to the fore, and mostly it was genuine. Her dress sense favoured 'sixties chic, encompassing gaudy, running colours and choosing materials that rarely seemed suited to one another but somehow went together well enough. Like leather and wool, or velvet and rubber. For an entire year she had gone barefoot, an act which brought no end of funny looks on the streets and in the Tube. She wore a red gypsy earring hoop through her left nostril, and it earned enough stares for her to add a second one, blue this time, to her lip. Her friends tolerated her with patient smiles and breathy sighs. She was an artist, after all; some quirks were only to be expected. The quirks were, however, mainly limited to her appearance. London was a game that she played well. Those in her circle expected exhibitions of strangeness, and there were obligations to be met. It was art imitating life imitating art.

And yet for all her surface compromise, her instincts remained wholly conservative. The men she dated, the occasional men, were strictly acceptable types; finely suited, stable in their outlook, men who tended towards the world of high finance or matters of law. They were typically well-mannered and immaculately groomed, and they knew how to treat a woman. She knew that they enjoyed the idea of being seen around town with someone like her on their arm, and she understood that way of thinking. With her, they could feel adventurous without ever really having to lay anything on the line. But when she let them take her to bed, finally, after the necessary four or five dates, often longer than that, their roles reversed, and it was they who turned wild while she found herself overcome by the plague of shyness. Intimacy was always so difficult for her.

That life felt an eternity from how she existed now. Here, there was none of London's excess. Most of the families who populated the island had set their roots here generations ago, back even to a time before records were kept. These people had neither time nor patience for the flippancies of a casual lifestyle. There was no need to walk barefoot on these roads, no need to dress in flamboyant fashion in order to make an impression; she could not have been more noticed if she tried. She was alien to the locals in every way, betrayed by all the details of her being, from the slow and ever so slightly judgemental precision of her accent to the very notion that she could make a living from painting pictures. Better than a living; that she could come into such serious wealth from the pursuit of what they saw as a trifling pass-time, nothing more. Everyone was polite to her, smiling if they met her on the road or passing a few words of conversation if they were in the queue behind or ahead of her in the post office or in the butchers shop, but there was never an open-armed embrace, never anything to suggest that she belonged here.

One night she undressed for bed without drawing the curtains. The bare light bulb's hundred watts felt harsh around her as she peeled off her blouse and her old paint-splattered denims and in her underwear drifted back and forth across the bedroom, busying herself with folding clothes, rearranging the stack of weary, dog-eared paper-backs that crowded the shelves of the corner bookcase, tending to the things that irritated a tired mind. She moved around the room, enjoying her freedom, carefully only to avoid the large square canvas that leaned against the wall behind the room door. It was her latest painting, unfin-ished, a layered sky over an empty foreground. She'd spent a couple of days trying to find the necessary motivation to tackle it, but it was a commissioned piece for somebody who wanted the work simply as a boast. She had accepted the October deadline and had already cashed and banked the cheque, of course. Now it was a piece of work, no longer even art, something better ignored.

Her bedroom window afforded a view all the way to the sea, and there were no houses to bother her, nothing but the tumble of open land. She hadn't looked to see if her visitor might have been watching from the hawthorn or even closer, because such confirmation would have made towers of her inhibitions. Juggling knowledge and denial fit perfectly into fantasy. Feigning distraction, she slipped from her black lace bra and, with a deep steadying breath, from her panties, then forced herself to bother again with the busy chore of folding clothes.

After a while she moved to the window and opened it, leaning out a little so that she might feel the night's fine breeze caress her face and breasts. When she caught sight of him down below, hunched low in the open part of the garden just where she liked to set up her easel, she looked quickly away and pretended instead to study the village in the near distance to the west, the reflecting lights of the houses and pubs setting alight the calm imposition of the harbour tide. Below her she could hear him breathing, that thin asthmatic rasp coming in fast spurts, and then that breathing broke into choking groans. Forced to look, she saw him drop to his knees and spill onto his side on the shorn grass, but rather than shame or frighten him, she pulled the window closed again, humming softly to herself the air of a fiddle tune she had picked up from somewhere, the murmur of it quivering in her throat, shaken in its time by the hard beat of her heart. A wave of self-loathing flushed through her, threatening darkness, and she pulled on an old oversized t-shirt, snapped off the light and crawled into bed to cry herself to sleep.

'Hello, Tadhg,' she said, startling him. He was sitting on the rocks down along where the seals tended to gather, a mile or so further east of the harbour, a peaceful place. She had watched him throwing stones out into the water, underarm, sending them out twenty-five or thirty yards with no effort at all.

'Isn't it a beautiful day?' The sun was mostly lost behind a marbled veneer of cloud, but the air was fresh and warm, pleasant for walking or for a picnic.

Tadhg stared at her, his mouth pulled into a gag in place of an answer. They had not been introduced, and he was not used to people speaking to him. She gazed out across the sea and let him stare. This part of the shoreline was sheltered by the cloaking rock walls of the low cliffs, but farther out a breeze was churning up the water, capping the bilge with froth. Gulls circled, watching for food, canting in and out of their own unconvincing rotation pattern.

'I've seen you around the island,' she said, smiling to herself as she watched the waves pull towards the rocks. 'My name is Marguerite, by the way. I have a place up on Broad Hill, but you probably know that. If there's one thing I've learned about this place it's that nothing much stays a secret around here for very long.'

He licked his lips and took to studying his hands. 'You're pretty,' he said, the first words she had heard him speak. His voice had a peculiar quality; deep and hoarse, yet soft, somehow. The accent accounted for some of that softness but there was something more too, rubbing away all edges. He sounded uncertain of his words; not used to speaking, she supposed. Certainly not used to speaking to a woman.

'Thank you,' she said, embarrassed and pleased.

Without waiting for an invitation, she found a place to sit on the rocks, close enough to seem friendly but still beyond the reach of anything but the most desperate lunge. A silence stretched out between them and became uncomfortable. He stopped throwing stones and stole glances at her with a certain rolling of his neck; meant as discreet, it was actually quite charming in its naivety. His eyes were the same pale and beautiful shade that she remembered, and she wondered if he was thinking about the way she had looked that night at the bedroom window. Today she was wearing a summer dress, sleeveless but still quite proper, and it was one of her favourites because she knew how much it flattered her, making a boast not only of her complexion but also of her body's shape.

'I love the sound of the sea,' he told her, his voice breaking. Marguerite was surprised to see tears tracing runnels down into the jagged red brush of stubble that mottled his jaws. She wanted to ask what was wrong, but the words seemed unnecessary. Edging closer, she touched his arm. It was the greatest gesture of comfort that she dared to make. Any sense of nervousness fell away when he flinched at the contact and, overcome by sympathy, she persevered, gently stroking his arm and uttering soft, nonsensical noises of consolation. The muscles of his forearm felt immense through the coarse wool of his shirtsleeve.

Time lost all thread of itself. Tadhg's face seemed to crumble, giving vent to what must have been years of pent-up strain, and he clenched his eyes shut and began to sob from somewhere deep within. Marguerite continued to mumble sounds of reassurance, easing her arm around him and whispering that it was good to cry sometimes, that he had nothing to be ashamed of and that he'd feel better once he had let it all out. When he folded his body towards her, embracing, she didn't hesitate. She could feel his heartbeat racing against her breast, and nothing but her whispered breath felt appropriate. The gloom that gripped the day was stifling, an avowal that the sun had been put away. The wind sighed out across the water as a judgement call. She had to battle to keep from shivering, though it was still warm, not yet five o'clock, a Sunday in early September. His arms held on as though they'd never let go, not hurting her exactly but ferocious just the same in their hinted strength. There was something wrong, she realised. The loneliness they shared had a diseased quality. She tried, as gently as she could to pull away from him, her left hand easing from his hunched back and dropping to straighten the skirt of her dress.

But he held her tight to him.

'I have to go, Tadhg,' she said, trying to project a sense of calm when her mind felt only like screaming. 'It's getting late and I have work to do. Please, Tadhg, let me go.' There was an instant when it seemed as though he would, and as she felt his grip loosen around her more words gushed to the surface, dramatically happy, false. 'I want us to be friends,' she told him. 'You're welcome to visit me any time. If you call, I'll show you some of my paintings, my best ones.' Feeling some need to explain, but nearly delirious at the thoughts of being away, and free. 'Maybe I'll even paint one for you.'

When the grip tightened around her again it was higher on her shoulders than before, those great strong arms crushing even as she tried to squeeze free. Tadhg held her that way for a long time after her neck had snapped, held her until dusk closed in and until he had cried himself out. Finally, he stood up and let her go. She slumped down onto the rocks, almost without a sound, slipped partially and then caught on some granite outcropping, so that she lay directly below him, perhaps five feet down, the waves lapping back over her splayed legs, their foaming edges pulling at her dress, offering him steady glimpses of her thighs and, occasionally, her buttocks hemmed in by the high cut of her black lace panties.

The tide would carry her away. People would wonder where she had gone, but she was a stranger to these parts. If they found her at all, if she somehow ended up tangled in some fisherman's nets, they'd decide that she had fallen on the rocks, or maybe jumped. That had been known to happen. No one would look too hard, though, not for an outsider. And no one would bother Tadhg about the matter. He sat a while and watched how the water lapped at her, and when the twilight began to take on the final sanguine tinge that often ushered in a late summer night on this island, he turned and traced a familiar path back up through the rocks towards the road.

IN THE DARKNESS

The boy, Jimmy, had been sleeping until he felt the narrow mattress shift away from him, and then suddenly he was wide awake, understanding everything. He had listened to the other boys talking about this, about how the priest came to visit them sometimes in the middle of the night, and about what he liked to do. The stories were so often discussed, either out on the hurling pitch where there was too much space for anyone in authority to overhear or during the stolen moments of morning recess, the fifteen-minute slice of freedom between the tyranny of Catechism Studies and the relentless grind of eleven o'clock Mathematics, that it was almost possible for Jimmy to imagine those terrible first touches of soft and dusty hands crawling over his private places, bothering him in a way no one ever had before.

He'd listened, feeling a sickness in his stomach, while the older boys told their tales, tried to describe how it had felt, first the touching and then the pain when all that touching led to other things. Some of the boys tried to be brave about it, laughing like it was nothing at all really, and they'd talk about afterwards when they'd squeeze their half-crown rewards in their palms hard enough to set an imprint of the coin's markings into their flesh. You could get a lot for a half crown, of course, enough Gobstoppers, Peggy's Legs and Dolly Mixtures to last you until next time, if you rationed them out with a bit of care. They laughed about that, but the laughter didn't reach their eyes at all, and it didn't soften that catch of pain and fear that quivered uncomfortably in their throats.

'Don't worry,' they'd say, those who displayed the most bravado, as they studied their huddled audience from behind the masks of frozen, gagging smiles. 'You'll all get a turn. The old boy likes to share the half crowns around.'

Tonight, Jimmy's turn had come.

The mattress banked, and for a moment he was sure that he would roll from his right side onto his back, and that maybe he'd keep on rolling, right out onto the waxy linoleum floor. But the sensation must have been heightened in his mind because he didn't roll, didn't really move much at all. The weight set itself carefully down, aided by a hand pressing on his upper arm, and then settled, but still Jimmy lay there, on his side, hardly breathing, keeping his eyes closed and thinking about what the other boys had said, how they described what happened.

He didn't have to look to know that the priest was there. That familiar smell was irresistible, the cloying mixture of drink and something sprayed, a fruity perfumed scent that seemed a little like apples but wasn't, and there was the faint buzz that tinged every slow exhalation. Father Moriarty was old, in his sixties at least, and he had fat cold hands that liked to touch the cheeks of his boys and to pat their shoulders as he spoke to them, sometimes liked to catch their hands and hold them tight while he urged them to confess their sins, insisting with that persuasive way of his that full confession was critical for the well-being of their souls, and that they shouldn't dare to keep anything back, especially the things that shamed them most, the impure thoughts, the way they liked to touch themselves sometimes, because God saw, heard and knew everything, and their efforts at deception would only serve to sadden Him. 'Go on, boy,' he'd say, his small yellow-flecked eyes hooded by the long red lashes and his wet mouth pursed into a pull-down smile that revealed a lower row of tiny rotten teeth. He looked like no one else that Jimmy had ever seen, that oversized head laden with milky excesses of flesh, a bluish rope of vein so prominent at his left temple, his small nose constantly flaring its nostrils. The smattering of red hair lay thinly across his pate in greased too-long strands that he rubbed into place a thousand times a day. He was God's messenger, he often told them. And God's messenger was never to be denied.

Every drawn breath kept a perfect tempo, each sigh matching the next and the last exactly, the canting squeak holding its place over and over, swinging steadily against the beat. Even with his eyes closed, Jimmy could imagine that frail buzz frosting the air of the cold night dormitory, spinning gossamer curlicues, and that pink tongue lapping wet the prayerful lips. But as the blanket began a slow descent he pushed the image of Father Moriarty away and tried to focus instead on how it had been last summer on that lovely week when his uncle from Scotland, his mother's brother, Brian O'Neill, had come to visit. Every morning at ten, Uncle Brian would be there in the hallway by the front offices, tall and thin, sallow-skinned, with a crew-cut of jet black hair and a shadow of beard that showed even an hour after the closest shave imaginable. A stranger made familiar by want as well as by blood, a man in his thirties who would look Jimmy over from head to toe and back again, smiling with pride and sadness in a way that wrinkled those deep green eyes almost shut, and then he'd hold out a hand with the promise of a day at the seaside, or a trip to the cinema, or maybe a walk in the woods. Brian knew everything there was to know about trees and wildlife, it seemed, but he knew all about boats too. He was a Marine Engineer in the Royal Navy; this week in Waterford, he explained, was so that he could reconnect with a few things he missed and maybe also put a few past troubles to rest. Jimmy was the spit of his poor mother, apparently. Brian said this over and over, that she had the same eyes and the same way of smiling, shyly, with a flash of pink rising across her cheeks and with her head tilted ever so slightly to the side. 'I swear to God, Jimmy. I'd have been able to pick you out of a crowd of a thousand once I saw you smiling like that,' he said, and Jimmy, listening to the comparisons being drawn between himself and a woman he knew only by name, had felt as though his heart was about to burst from his chest with pride and joy.

The beat of the breathing behind him shifted, the wheeze becoming more pronounced, and the big cold hand was at him, no longer merely resting on his arm but touching him thoroughly, first through his clothes and then, when that was no longer enough, pulling at the waistband of his underpants, wrestling it down around his bare thighs. Without the blanket to cover him Jimmy could feel the hard caress of the chill night air lapping at him, drawing his flesh rigid and mottling it with a rash of goose pimples. The elastic of his underpants had twisted and was pressing an uncomfortable knot into the side of his left knee. He could have reached down and straightened it but didn't, and instead the irritation grew and grew. Later, in his nightmares or when he thought back on tonight, this first time, that piece of elastic would hold a lot of his mind's focus.

A moment of stillness stretched out, interminable and compromised only by the chase of his heart beating something that was equal parts terror and confusion high up in his chest, clenching at his throat muscles and nearly choking him, and then the hand was back, even colder than before, and more determined, and now there was nothing to protect him at all, not even the thin veil of cotton, not from God's messenger.

Guttural whispers flushed against the left side of his face, sometimes shaping his name, mostly settling for nonsensical urgings as the hand continued to forage. Tonight, God knew his name.

Uncle Brian talked a lot about growing up. There were only certain words now that hinted at his Waterford roots. He had left home at sixteen, he said. The Navy was some life, all right. 'They made a man of me, Jimmy. Educated me, trained me for a life at sea, helped me to build character.' He was tall and thin, but it was a wiry thinness, exuding strength. He had a girl, he said, Kathleen. She lived in Glasgow but of course they wouldn't live there after they were married. He'd want to be by the coast, he said, but not a city. A small town. Maybe Scotland, maybe even Ireland. Kathleen's blood was Irish, she had lovely long black hair and blue eyes. The grey photograph that he pulled from his wallet didn't give up much in the way of details but Jimmy could see that she was pretty, beautiful even, and it was easy to imagine the rest. 'A city is no place to bring up kids,' Brian said, tucking the photo safely back into the leathery folds of his wallet, in beside some identification documents and some crisp English pound notes. 'After we're married, we'll settle in a small town by the sea and set about starting ourselves a family. And Kathleen is a nurse, so she'll never have trouble finding work.' Jimmy had started into dreaming just about then, building in his mind a fantasy jigsaw-puzzle world of how it could be, not just for the loving couple but for them all. That grey photograph showed a kindly face, the trace of a smile stirring every feature to life. A motherly smile, he assured himself, one full of compassion, and of course he'd be no trouble to them at all, he'd be on his very best behaviour from now on and he'd never give them a single cause to worry about him or to regret giving him the chance of a family life.

For six days he held such thoughts as strictly secret until the Sunday, the final day of Brian's stay before returning to Scotland, Kathleen and the Royal Navy. They sat at one of the stained oak picnic tables set just off the strand at Ardmore, shielded from the worst of the breeze by the low dunes, and Jimmy was unfolding the tinfoil wrapping of the ham and cheese sandwiches while Brian measured out tea from a red flask into two small paper cups. They'd taken the bus from Dunmore East, sitting side by side, with Jimmy in the window seat and smiling at everything, unbearably happy, and Brian pointing out various passing things of interest, such as the horse chestnut trees that lined the roadside, the breeds of cattle in the fields, a stream that he knew to be especially good for trout, even the ruins of a round tower with the stubs of fallen stone blocks poking like bleached headstones up through the stringy waves of grass. When finally they arrived at the beach Jimmy had run straight to the water, pulling off his shoes at a hopping run that looked awkward and ridiculous and pitching them away one and then the other, before wading out to knee-deep in the freezing tide. Brian sauntered after him, laughing heartily at the shrieks of how cold the water was, and he stooped, gathered up the discarded shoes then dropped lazily onto the sand, now and again flapping the air around his face to ward off the irritation of a couple of scrambling flies but mostly fixing his stare on the horizon and the single slow drift of a trawler at work. It was a typically sunless day with temperatures in the mid-teens, and the cloaked light shifted as restlessly as the tide, waxing in and out of dreary gloom. None of that mattered to Jimmy, though. And after an hour or so of wading and splashing, the coldness of the water finally became unbearable and they decided that now would be a good time to eat the sandwiches.

'Could I come and live with you, Brian?' He hadn't meant to blurt it out so plainly, had rehearsed in his mind how he would work the question into conversation after he had made it clear how much sense it made, and how much of a help he could be to them. 'After you and Kathleen are married, I mean,' he added, shyly.

'Well,' said Brian, after he had carefully chewed and swallowed a bite of his sandwich. Some of the sandwiches had mustard, some didn't, and a speck of yellow freckled the corner of his mouth. He swabbed at it with his tongue, missed, and gave up. 'Would you really want to leave Ireland? I mean, all the friends you have here and all?'

'I would,' Jimmy said. He had dreamed of this conversation going differently and there was a sense that he'd lost his grip on things. But then something in his uncle's face seemed to soften.

'I'll discuss it with Kathleen, so. She doesn't know you, of course, but she's a lovely soul. I'll tell her you're my nephew, explain to her about your situation and about my poor misfortunate sister, the Lord have mercy on her, and it'll be fine, I'm sure of it. But you do understand that with me being tied up with the blasted Navy my time is not my own. It will be a year anyway before we can get married, maybe even two if house prices keep going up the way they're going. I expect to be away from home quite a lot for the foreseeable future, trying to get as many hours served as I can, do some serious saving. But it'll be no longer than two years, that much I'm sure of.' He gave a wry smile that seemed to say, *I doubt Kathleen will wait any longer than two years anyway*. Then he finished his sandwich with a flourish and asked Jimmy how that sounded. Jimmy, trying to pick the best threads from the wreckage, said that sounded just fine, and there was plenty of time in the weeks after to play the conversation over and over in his mind until it found a different slant, with all trace of negativity having fallen away.

'And in the meantime, we can keep in touch. You can write a letter, can't you?'

What else could Jimmy do but nod that, yeah, he could write just fine.

The other boys were right about the pain, but what they had said didn't even begin to describe it. Father Moriarty leaned in, one arm wrapped tightly around Jimmy's stomach, his breath spinning up in sharp, frenzied gasps. The night felt full of music, the iron railing of the bed frame's head keeping an unsteady time against the wall while the priest unfurled a relentless canticle of moans. Helpless to move, every riven thrust sending pain tearing through his body and his mind, Jimmy held his breath and tried to think of anything but what was happening now. This was late September and he had written three letters since the summer without yet receiving a reply. Uncle Brian was probably at sea, putting in the long hours, saving for their future. Tears squeezed from his clenched eyelids and slipped sideways over the bridge of his nose. Then the music of the night increased and he felt something break, down below and deep inside, and he opened his eyes to the conch of the bone-white moon that filled the upper corner of the dormitory's casement window, and waited for the end to come, for death.

The moon glowed in the frosted glass, but he understood that ten-year-old boys didn't die, not even from this. It was dark now but soon it would be morning, another day of lessons and hurling. Maybe he'd be excused sports, maybe not. Another day, a day like all the rest. And another day meant other nights. The priest began to whisper something, that big sweating head pressing down into the crook of his neck, that mouth with its sticky too-red lips lapping at his flesh, but he found a way to block all of that out by focusing on the weekend. He'd take his half crown down to Mrs O'Donoghue's and spend the whole thing on bars of Fry's Chocolate Cream and a bag of iced caramels and he'd eat them all at once, right there on the street, just gorge until he was sick.

NO ROOM AT THE INN

See the child, the infant boy wrapped in rags, huddled in his mother's arms, helpless in some doorway. The baby sleeps and sometimes cries, with cold or hunger, or sorrow for the world into which he has been born, for the life that he has been cursed, not blessed, to live.

His mother is just a child herself, probably not more than seventeen or eighteen. She is pretty in simple ways, but it is a prettiness without edge, the best things about her worn down. The doorway is her home for now, their home until the moment or the hour comes when they are moved on. She watches passers-by, hoping for and dreading a glimpse of a face she knows. Her heart slaps with fear as men approach, glance at her and then quickly glance away, their eyes heavy with shame and disgust.

Rain washes clean the streets but at a cost of comfort. Most people hunch their shoulders and hurry along, laden with bags of senseless impulses, their faces all the same; expressions tight and stretched by imagined stress, bubbles of rage and frustration contorting their features. Christmas is a trying time.

A rattle of coins fall into the paper cup. The young mother raises her eyes and smiles a tired, aching smile of gratitude, but the giver is already gone, just another raincoat in the sea of shoppers. The coins mix with the watery dregs of cold tea, small but welcome, something but never enough.

The child wakes and, cradled tightly in his mother's arms, watches the ropes of Christmas lights sway gently high above the street. Reds, yellows and blues, balls of colour against the drab smear of stormy sky beyond. He watches, transfixed at their brightness, the seasonal colours, maybe the colours of heaven. After awhile, there is for him the suddenness of something fearful, illogical maybe but clear, and he cries, his breath gasping and bronchial. But his voice is drowned out by the goodwill-to-all-men call seeping from the warmth of a shop, *Silver Bells* or *Silent Night*, and the passers-by hurry along, leaving the mother to whisper the nonsensical securities that gradually quell the tears.

Rain gives every breath a dampness, a down-and-out city taste. To the busy people trampling the streets, it is the tang of inconvenience, the shrug that seems to say, 'Well, it wouldn't be Christmas shopping without a little discomfort'. But to those already down, the homeless and cast aside, it is not merely the taste of inconvenience but of existence.

Someone else drops a few coins, throwaway pence, a middle-aged woman, her head all but hidden in a scarf. She doesn't hurry past but waits to collect her thank-you smile. But at least she stopped; many hurry past, and if they glance at mother and child at all it is to share a look of disgust, their faces pinched with disapproval. The look that kicks and keeps on kicking. 'I'd give them nothing,' they'll tell any who will listen. 'They'd only put it to drink.'

Maybe they don't realise that, for a little while, drink can replace a roaring fire or chase away the fear that sits with our most vulnerable. Or maybe they just don't care.

A Christmas Eve knows early darkness. When the streets quiet and that voice comes, 'All right, move it along now,' mother and child are disturbed into motion. To try the shelters, though the shelters are usually full at winter time; to walk away the hours of Eve to Day, perhaps stealing minutes of sleep in some other vacant doorway. Maybe they will be all right, mother and child, maybe there is still a way up from here, or a way out. Maybe the infant boy will grow up to be a man, a somebody, a king. Maybe he will change the world; it happened once before, so why not again?

FOR THE LOVE OF YOLANDA

Garnet Tock wades from the sheltering line of firs out into the centre of a field and stops to listen, but dawn breaks without a sound across the valley. There is nothing to be heard, not the whine of a breeze, no screaming birds, not the scrabbling of rodents or small animals, and certainly not a despairing bark. The sky presses low, gleaming even in this hinted light, layer upon layer of cloud bruised opaque with menace, the next onslaught of snow feeling little more than a gasp away.

When he can bear the inaction no longer, he trudges forward, afraid both of what he might find and of what might elude him. The rifle in his gloved hands has killed often and well, but never has he needed it more than now, and for the comfort of its rage as much as for its ability to bring down whatever settles in its sights. Animals, yes, necessary for his survival, but men too, twice over the past few years and several more back when he had been in Vietnam. This morning he will kill if he is forced to do so, and peace of mind will lie no further than a prayer of contrition away. Out here the ferocious survive and the weak grow hungry, so killing is like taking breakfast or cutting wood: just a part of the day. And out here the rifle is his friend and confidant, granting assurance that he will be able to do whatever needs doing.

As he cleaves a furrow through the snow the land folds away from him in a spreading vista. Patchwork shades of grey are broken apart only by the black mesh of briars but there is no movement anywhere. His breath seeps from his mouth, forced audible with effort, spinning thin grey spools that hang in the bitter air, then vanish slowly. When he laps at his chapped lips he tastes the salt of his own blood. This year he has developed a wheeze, just a tenor-touch to the most extreme edge of every exhalation, but he knows without wanting to that it represents the little pinched discomfort that has become an ever-present feature down his right side, that lung weakened ever since a bout of childhood pneumonia and now inching towards something even worse.

'Yolanda!' His voice is desperate with pleading whenever he shouts her name, a worn stub of a voice that echoes in flapping waves out across the land. But he receives no reply, and has mostly given up expecting one.

It would have been difficult for anybody or anything to survive a night exposed to these elements, and impossible surely for a wolfhound bitch used to the shelter of a log cabin, to eating what is put before her and to curling up before a well-set fire. Maybe she had enough about her to take shelter that first night after they were separated by the quick tumble of darkness, but this is now the sixth day since she'd strayed and gotten herself lost. There are other men out in this country, not settled close, but they could have hooked themselves on a trail while hunting deer or even quail and easily crossed into this valley. A blaze of heat spouts up in Garnet's chest, a stew of anger, fear and frustration.

Yolanda is five-years-old now, and the companion of his

life, having been hand-raised from a raw pup. He chose the name in memory of a girl he had known in his youth, a fair sort who had once teased him to a frenzy but who damaged him nearly fatally when, while laughing and making eyes at someone else, she dropped him from a height. There are always some wounds that feel as though they will never heal, but then time takes hold and turns its tricks. His cuts were deep but with the right kind of nursing he found a way through, and he can finally holler the name now without fearing the ache of memory. There is only one Yolanda for him, he tells himself often, only one that matters.

Hours pass. He trudges along through fields he knows, and then, less sure of himself, onto land that looks the same as all the rest but is new to him, and he stops only when the pain slashes harder into his side. He surveys the landscape then, bites off a nip of cheap corn whiskey from a dented tin hipflask and savours the crawling tendrils of heat that bloom in his chest. The sun climbs in a slow arc but never shows as anything more than a pale smear through the shellac screed of cloud. What snow has fallen crunches underfoot, fine white motes densely packed from months of falling. Occasional flurries continue to slake the air, cautious smatterings that hint of worse to come. He understands, though, that he has no choice but to ignore the warning.

Noon slips by. He has walked for miles and the day is reaching that point where he will have to turn back soon or else risk the darkness and the possibility of getting lost. He is hungry and tired, and his side is hurting, his breath reduced down to stuttering gasps by the cold and the strain of this hunt. One more day is all that he can allow, and then he will have to give Yolanda up as lost. Tomorrow it will have been a week since she strayed. His mind plays the usual tricks, drawing visions of her tall sleek shape cantering towards him, the dark gleam of her eyes fixed on his and yearning for some show of affection, her lean haunches matted in wild tufts of dirty copper-red hair, that great tongue lolling from the right of her yawning mouth and heaving with joyous ropes of froth from too much running. There is a second image too, the image of her lying hurt, and though he tries to keep this to the periphery it remains a nagging presence amongst his thoughts. The idea of her lovely shape ruined by some claw trap or a hateful bullet, waiting for the peace of death while dark geysers of her blood spout and then trickle from the hole in her neck to pollute the snow, fills him with terror.

The dash of something fast and grey flickers along the very fringe of his vision and is just as quickly lost. He studies the land to his left, focusing on the jagged bucktooth poke of rocks that lie perhaps a thousand yards away. His heart is pounding, but he only allows himself a second of doubt because the best of the day is already gone and there is no time for hesitation. He grips the rifle across his chest and stumbles out to investigate, this direction as good as any other. There are wolves here in this valley, the sort of huge grey beasts that even a rifle's bullet cannot be counted on to stop.

Up around the blue granite outcroppings, the terrain is rough and broken, and the snow has been unable to bank with enough mass to hold tracks. Garnet struggles over a cleft of rock to find a small creek lying in wait. A thread of water chases in ribbons through the coloured stones of the riverbed, just a few determined inches at its widest point and penned in by frozen walls but using the incline to keep from fully icing over. Glassy spumes of fog hang above, the pervading cold brutalising the disturbed air. He finds a sheltered hollow in the rocks and settles down to wait. Something else is here.

A scrabble of dirt snaps him awake. He is shocked to discover that night has almost fallen, and now there can be no attempt at making it back to the cabin. Snow is falling again, chill wisps drifting like feathers through the twilit air. They nestle on his shoulders and in his hair and hold their shapes. The sound of movement comes from the far side of the creek, but the jut of the rocks conceal whatever it is that begins to lap at the chasing stream's ice water. He listens, hoping that he will be able to tell by the weight of the footfall whether it is Yolanda or something he will have to gun down, but after a few seconds it becomes clear to him that no such simple identity is possible. Shifting as silently as his stiff muscles and frozen bones will allow, he raises his rifle and then crawls towards a crevice in the rock.

Wolf. That is his first thought, but then the creature raises its head from the ripple of the stream and even through the tumble of first darkness Garnet sees that it isn't a wolf at all but a dog. He watches as it stretches its back and raises its head, smelling at the cold air, catching perhaps some hint of danger even through the searing cold. It is large in size, its thick coat mottled with dabs of dark grey over a pale underlining.

He can't determine the breed type and decides that it is not strictly a breed at all but some mix of nature and circumstance that has somehow found a way of surviving out here, foraging for food and battling the cold. Then a second movement stirs the dark bank and Yolanda moves with graceful caution to the water. The pair are clearly comfortable together. While Yolanda drinks, the dog looms protectively beside her and then she rises and nuzzles against him, sharing warmth and maybe love too.

Garnet raises the rifle and draws the big dog's shoulder into his sights. The cold has shut down his mind; he uses his teeth to draw the glove from his right hand and feels nothing at all as he squeezes the trigger. A flare of light sparks in the darkness and the dog crumbles on the stony bank, and for just a moment the air swims thickly with the tarrying bark and peppering gunpowder stench of the shot. It is instinct that causes Yolanda to charge for cover, but it is something else that makes her stop just a few yards away and then nervously return to where her mate lies twitching. When Garnet rises from his hiding place she turns to look at him, and when he calls her and she doesn't respond he tells himself that she is just afraid. He climbs down and traces a way across the stream. Yolanda lowers her head and backs away just a step. He smiles at her then drops into a crouch beside the shot dog and strokes the animal's wiry coat until the slow efforts at breathing subsides to nothing.

'You look hungry,' he says, when the silence becomes uncomfortable. From his pocket his pulls a strand of deer jerky, considers splitting it and then tosses it towards her. She stares at him, then snaps it up and begins to chew. When she finishes he smiles again. Night has fallen and they really need to find some shelter, but suddenly he feels as though he can make it back to the cabin.

'Come on, Yolanda,' he says. 'Let's get you home.'

She hesitates for just an instant, and then surrenders.